Gil Addison Showed A Definite Talent For Stripping.

If he'd undressed any slower, Bailey would've ripped the shirt off. But she had asked for this. All she could do was watch in torment.

With her training, Bailey could bring most men down. But Gil...Gil was the real deal. His body rippled with muscle.

"Cat got your tongue?" he taunted.

Her legs shaking, she curled her arm around the bedpost. "Just admiring the view." She touched his chest. "I want to please you."

"You do, in every way. I love your strength, your integrity. The way you treat my son."

"He's lucky to have you."

His finger on her lips silenced her. "I spend all my time being Cade's father. Tonight...tonight I'm just a man. A man who wants you."

Beneath
the Stetson

JANICE
MAYNARD

MILLS
BOON®

Published in Great Britain 2014
by Mills & Boon, an imprint of Harlequin (UK) Limited,
Large Print edition 2014
Eton House, 18-24 Paradise Road,
Richmond, Surrey, TW9 1SR

© 2014 by Harlequin Books S.A.

Special thanks and acknowledgment to Janice Maynard for her contribution to the Texas Cattleman's Club: The Missing Mogul miniseries.

ISBN: 978 0 263 24420 5

Harlequin (UK) Limited's policy is to use papers that are natural, renewable and recyclable products and made from wood grown in sustainable forests. The logging and manufacturing processes conform to the legal environmental regulations of the country of origin.

Printed and bound in Great Britain
by CPI Antony Rowe, Chippenham, Wiltshire

JANICE MAYNARD

is a *USA TODAY* bestselling author who lives in beautiful east Tennessee with her husband. She holds a B.A. from Emory and Henry College and an M.A. from East Tennessee State University. In 2002 Janice left a fifteen-year career as an elementary school teacher to pursue writing full-time. Now her first love is creating sexy, character-driven, contemporary romance stories.

Janice loves to travel and enjoys using those experiences as settings for books. Hearing from readers is one of the best perks of the job! Visit her website, www.janicemaynard.com, and follow her on Facebook and Twitter.

For my wonderful Texas friends,
Karen, Rob, Elaine and Bob.
Thank you for the fun, the laughter
and the "tall" tales of life in Texas.
I count you among my blessings!

One

Gil Addison didn't like Feds. Even when they came wrapped in pretty packages. Perhaps it was the trace of Comanche blood in his veins that kept an atavistic memory alive...all those years of government promises made and broken. Gil was a white man living in a white man's world, no doubt about it. Nothing much of his Native American heritage lingered except for his black hair, brown eyes and olive skin.

But the distrust remained.

He stood inside the house, hand on an edge of the curtain, and watched as a standard-issue dark sedan made its way down the long drive-way. Technically, the woman for whom he waited wasn't a Fed. She was a state investigator. But she had been trained by Feds, and that was close enough.

"Who is it, Daddy?"

His four-year-old son, Cade, endlessly curious, wrapped an arm around his father's leg. Gil glanced down at the boy, smiling in spite of his unsettled emotions. "A lady who wants to talk to me. Don't worry. It won't take long." He had promised Cade they would go riding today.

"Is she pretty?"

Gil raised an eyebrow. "Why would that matter?"

The child with the big, far-too-observant eyes grinned. "Well, if she is, you might want to date her and fall in love and then get married and—"

"This again?" Gil kept his hand over the boy's mouth in a mock insistence on changing the subject. He knelt and looked Cade in the eyes. "I have you. That's all I need." Single parenting was not for wimps. Sometimes it was the loneliest job in the world. And Gil wondered constantly if he was making irrevocable mistakes. He hugged his son before standing up again. "I think I've been letting you watch too much TV."

Cade pulled the curtains even farther aside and watched as the car rolled to a stop and parked. The car door opened and the woman stepped out. "She *is* pretty," Cade said, practically bouncing with the energy that never seemed to diminish.

Inwardly, Gil agreed with Cade's assessment, albeit reluctantly. Bailey Collins, despite the professional pantsuit that was as dark and unexceptional as her car, made an impression on a man. Only a few inches shy of Gil's six-one height, she carried herself with confidence. Wavy, shoulder-length brown hair glinted in the sun with red highlights. Her thick-lashed eyes were almost as dark as Gil's.

Though she was still too far away for Gil to witness those last two attributes, he had a good memory. Today was not his first encounter with Bailey Collins.

As she mounted his front steps, he opened the door, refusing to acknowledge that his heart beat faster than normal. The first time he met her, they had faced each other across a desk at Royal's police station. Even then he'd felt a potent mix of sexual hunger and resentment. But Bailey was on his turf now. He'd be calling the shots. She might think her credentials gave her power, but he was not prepared to accept them at face value.

Bailey caught her toe on the edge of the top step and stumbled, almost falling flat on her face. Fortunately, she regained her balance at the last second, because in the midst of her gyrations the door flew open, and a man she recognized all too well stood framed in the doorway.

Gil Addison.

Even as she acknowledged the jolt to her chest, she was taken aback by the presence of a second male. The man for whom she felt an unwelcome but visceral attraction was not alone. He held the hand of a small boy, most likely—according to Gil's dossier—his son. Even without written verification, she could have guessed the relationship. The young one was practically a carbon copy of his older counterpart.

The child broke free of his father's hold and stepped forward to beam at Bailey. "Welcome to the Straight Arrow," he said, holding out his hand with poignant maturity. His gap-toothed smile was infectious. "I'm Cade."

Bailey squatted, holding out her hand, as well,

feeling the warmth of the small palm as it nestled briefly in hers. "Hello, Cade," she said. "I'm Bailey."

"Ms. Collins," Gil corrected with a slight frown. "I'm trying to teach him manners."

"It's not bad manners to use my first name if I offer the privilege," Bailey said evenly, rising to face the man who had already given her sleepless nights.

Cade looked back and forth between the two adults. The thinly veiled antagonism between them was unfortunate, because Cade seemed first confused and then unhappy. The boy's chin wobbled. "I wanted my dad to like you," he whispered, staring up at Bailey with huge blue eyes that must have come from his mother.

Bailey's heart melted. "Your dad and I like each other just fine," she told Cade, daring Gil to disagree. "Sometimes grown-ups get frustrated about things, but that doesn't mean we're angry." Even as an adult of thirty-three, she remembered vague impressions of her parents arguing. Yelling. Saying wretched, bitter words that couldn't be unheard.

Bailey knew what it was like to be a child with

no power to shape the course of events. It was because she *did* understand Cade's dismay, that she summoned an almost-genuine smile and aimed it in Gil's direction. "Thank you for seeing me today. If we can sit down for a few moments, I promise not to take up too much of your time."

With Cade standing squarely in between them, there was nothing for Gil to do but agree. He ruffled his son's hair, love for his child and wry capitulation in his gaze as he spoke. "Why don't you join us in the kitchen, Ms. Collins? Cade and I usually have lemonade and a snack right about now."

"You may as well call me Bailey, too," she muttered, not sure if he heard her or not. She followed the two of them back through the house to the historic but updated kitchen. Gil had taken over the property from his parents when they retired and settled in Austin. The senior Addisons had inherited the Straight Arrow from Gil's grandparents. The ranch, whose name ironically described its owner to a T, was an enormous operation.

Four years ago when Gil's wife committed suicide, Gil had hired an army of extra ranch hands and housekeepers, so he could be the primary caregiver for his toddler son. Bailey knew the facts of the situation because she had investigated the man…and admired him for his devotion. But that didn't make her any more forgiving of the way he had stonewalled her in their earlier interviews. Even though her file on Gil Addison was thorough and extensive, she was no closer to understanding the man himself.

Cade pulled out a chair for Bailey, sealing the deal. The kid was irresistible. Clearly Gil was not kidding when he mentioned teaching manners. Something about witnessing the boy's interaction with his father made Bailey's assessment of Gil shift and refocus. Surely a man who could be so caring and careful with a child was not all bad.

Bailey's own exposure to male parenting was more like a metaphorical slap up the side of the head. *Toe the line. Don't complain. Achieve. Be self-sufficient.* Even the most generous assessment of her father's motives left no room for seeing him as anything other than a bully and a tyrant—presumably the reason Bailey's mother had walked out, leaving her young daughter behind.

Bailey sat down somewhat self-consciously,

and placed her cell phone on the table. While Gil busied himself retrieving glasses from the pine cabinets and slicing apples to go along with peanut butter, Cade grilled Bailey. "Do you have any good games on your phone?"

His hopeful expression made her grin. "A few."

"Angry Birds?"

"Yes. Are you any good at it?"

Cade shot a glance at his dad and lowered his voice. "He thinks that too much time with electronics will make me…um…" Clearly searching for the desired word, Cade trailed off, his brow furrowed.

"Brain dead." Gil set the glasses on the table and returned with the plate of apples. Taking a chair directly across from Bailey, he sat down and turned his son's hand over, palm up. The little fingers were grimy. "Go wash up, Cade. Ms. Collins and I will wait for you."

When Cade disappeared down the hall to the bathroom, Bailey smiled. "He's wonderful. And unexpectedly mature for a four-year-old."

"He'll be five soon. He didn't have too many opportunities to be around other children until I began bringing him to the daycare center at the club occasionally, so that accounts for the adult conversation. As much as I'll miss him, I think it will be good for him to start kindergarten this fall."

Bailey cocked her head. "I may have misjudged you, Gil Addison. I think you *do* have a heart."

"Don't confuse parental love for weakness, Ms. Collins. I won't be manipulated into helping you take down one of my friends."

The sudden attack startled her. Gil's classic features were set in grim lines, any trace of softness gone. "You really don't trust me at all, do you?" she asked, her voice husky with regret at this evidence of his animosity.

"I don't trust your kind," he clarified, his tone terse. "Alex Santiago was kidnapped, but now he's been found. Sooner or later he'll get his memory back and be able to tell us who took him. Why can't you people drop it and leave us here in Royal to clean up our own messes?"

Bailey glanced toward the hallway, realizing that Cade could return at any moment. "Surely you're not that naive," she said quietly. "Because Alex has no memory of what happened to him, trouble could strike again at any time. We have no choice but to track down his abductors. Surely you can see that."

"What I don't see is why you think anyone I know is responsible."

"Alex was well-liked in Royal, though obviously he had at least one enemy. *You* know a lot of people. Somewhere in the midst of all that I hope to find the truth. It's my job, Gil. And I'm good at it. All I need is your help."

Cade popped into the room, the front of his shirt damp from his ablutions. "I'm really hungry," he said. At a nod from his father, he scooped up two apple slices and started eating.

As Bailey watched, Gil offered her a piece and took one himself. His sharp white teeth bit into the fruit with a crunch. She tried to eat, but the food stuck in her throat. She needed Gil on her side. And she needed him to trust her. Perhaps that would require time.

Biting her lip, she put down her uneaten snack and tried the lemonade instead. As father and son chatted about mundane matters, she strove for composure. Usually it took a lot to rattle her. But for some reason, winning Gil's approval was important.

When his phone rang, he glanced at the number and grimaced. "Sorry, Ms. Collins. I need to take this in private. I won't be long."

Cade glanced up at his dad as Gil stood. "Don't worry, Daddy. I'll entertain her."

When Gil returned thirty minutes later, he felt a pinch of guilt for abandoning Bailey to his son's clutches. Not all women were good with children, and Bailey struck him as more of a focused career woman than a nurturer. When he crossed the threshold into the kitchen, he pulled up short. There at the table, right where he had left them, were Cade and Bailey. Only now, they were sitting side by side, their heads bent over Bailey's phone.

The lemonade glasses were empty, as was the plate that had held apples.

Bailey shook her head. "Remember the angles," she said. "Don't just fire it off willy-nilly."

When Gil's son gazed up at Bailey, Gil's heart fractured. Never had he seen a boy so starved for feminine attention. Despite Gil's best efforts at being a perfect parent, nothing could substitute for the love of a mother. If Gil were not careful,

Cade would latch onto Bailey and create an embarrassing situation for all of them.

Gil cleared his throat. "Cade. If you'll give me half an hour to speak with Ms. Collins about some grown-up business, I promise you we'll leave for our ride immediately after that."

Cade never looked up from his game. "Sure, Dad. Let me just finish this one—"

Gil took the phone and handed it to Bailey. "You have permission to use the computer in my study. Now scram."

"Yes, sir." Cade gave Bailey a cheeky grin on his way out the door. "Will you say goodbye before you leave?"

Bailey rose to her feet and glanced at Gil.

Cade's father nodded. "I'll let you know when we're done."

In Cade's absence an uncomfortable silence reigned. The little boy's exuberant personality had served to soften the edges of Gil's aggressive displeasure.

Bailey hesitated, searching for a way to break the ice.

Gil did it for her. He held out an arm. "Since Cade is in my office, we might as well step onto the back porch. If that's okay with you," he added stiffly.

Bailey nodded. "Of course." The January weather was picture-perfect, and as was often the case during the winter, a bit erratic, as well. Last week Royal had endured storms and temperatures in the mid-fifties. Today the thermometer was forecast to hit eighty, almost a record.

As they stepped outside, Bailey had to smile. The Straight Arrow was an enormous, thriving cattle operation. In addition to its efficiency and profitability, every aspect of the ranch's physical appearance was neat and aesthetically pleasing to the eye. It took money to carry out such attention to detail. But Gil had money. Lots of it. Which was a good thing, because his wealth meant he had the luxury of spending time with his son.

Watching and listening to Cade, Bailey understood how very well Gil had managed to give his son emotional security. The child was bright, friendly and well adjusted. Growing up without a mother was no picnic. But Gil's parenting had mitigated Cade's loss as much as was possible.

Gil remained standing, so Bailey followed suit. If she had made herself comfortable in one of the cushioned wicker chairs, he would have towered over her. She suspected he would like that.

Bailey, however, had a job to do. She wouldn't be cowed by Gil's fiercely masculine personality. She worked in a world where men still dominated the profession. Self-preservation demanded she be tough on the outside, even if she sometimes felt as if she was playing a part.

Gil fired the first shot. "I thought you went back to Dallas."

She shrugged. "Only for a week. The case is still open. After I finished the earlier interviews, my boss pulled me to work briefly on another project. But we're in a lull now, and they want me to do some more digging."

"You didn't do so well the last time," he mocked.

Bailey met his hot gaze with composure. "Investigations take time. And just so you know…I get it, Gil."

"Get what?"

"You were insulted to be on the suspect list. I impugned your honor, and you're pissed. Have I hit the nail on the head?" She challenged him deliberately, not willing to play the bad guy indefinitely.

His jaw was granite. "I'd think your time would be better spent questioning the criminal element instead of harassing upstanding members of the community."

Her lips twitched. Hurt masculine pride was a tricky thing. "I have extensive training in psychological evaluation. And you know very well that you were never a suspect. It was my job to speak to anyone and everyone who knew Alex… to look for clues, for any shred of information, no matter how minute, that might help solve the kidnapping."

"And yet you came up with nothing."

She tensed, tired of being under attack. "Alex is back in Royal," she pointed out.

"No thanks to you."

His mockery lit the fuse of her temper. She could take what he was dishing out, but she didn't have to like it. "You have no idea what goes on behind the scenes. And I don't have to justify myself to you. Can we please get back to the matter at hand?"

"And that would be?"

As they had exited the house, Gil had scooped up a well-worn Stetson and dropped it on his head with one smooth motion that bespoke the love of a cowboy for his hat. Now the brim shadowed his eyes.

Bailey was not immune to the picture he made. In well-washed denims that rode low on his hips and molded to his long, muscular legs, he was a walking, talking ad for testosterone. His chamois shirt must have been hand-tailored, because it managed to accommodate his broad shoulders nicely. Gil Addison was the real deal, right down to his expensive, though scuffed, leather boots.

Bailey felt the physical pull. Acknowledged it. Experienced a pang of regret for something that would never be. It had been a long time since she had met a man so appealing. But Gil didn't much like her, and her newest assignment was not going to improve matters.

With an inward sigh for her barren love life, she cut to the chase. "I need access to the membership files at the Texas Cattleman's Club."

"Absolutely not." He bowed up almost visibly.

Bailey leaned against the porch railing, her hands behind her. It was either that or fasten them around Gil's tanned neck and squeeze. The man was infuriating. "I have all the necessary warrants and paperwork," she said mildly. "But I'd prefer not to go in guns blazing. Why don't you be a gentleman for once and politely invite me to the club as your guest?"

The word he muttered made her wince. "I'm the *president* of the TCC," he pointed out…as if she didn't already know. His scowl was black. "People trust me with their secrets. How is it going to look if I turn all that over to an outsider?"

That last jab hurt, but Bailey held her ground. "You don't really have a choice…even if you do have a judge or two tucked away in your back pocket. These orders come down from on high. I'm going to comb through those files one way or another. You can either make my life miserable or you can cooperate. Your choice. But I *will* get the information I need."

Two

Gil ripped his hat from his head and ran a hand across his damp brow. It was January, damn it. No reason in the world the heat and humidity should be this bad.

Bailey, on the other hand, despite wearing an unflattering suit jacket, seemed cool and collected. She watched him warily, as if he were a dangerous rattlesnake about to bite.

What she didn't know was that he *had* fantasized about nibbling her…all the way from her delicate jawline to the vulnerable place where her throat disappeared inside that boring blouse. His body tightened. The woman probably had no idea that her no-nonsense clothing revved his engine.

Instead of focusing on the government-employee quasi uniform, he imagined stripping it off her and baring that long, lean body to his gaze.

His sex thickened and lifted, making his jeans uncomfortably tight. With a silent curse, he stared out across the acres of land that belonged to him as far as the eye could see. Searching desperately for a diversion, he fell back on the universal topic of weather.

"Are you familiar with the Civil War general Philip Sheridan?" he asked, keeping his body half-turned to avoid embarrassing them both.

Bailey wrinkled her nose. "History wasn't my strong suit in school, but yes…I've heard of him."

"After the war, Sheridan was assigned to a post in south Texas. It's reported he said that if he owned Texas and hell, he would rent out Texas and live in hell."

"I'm surprised you would mention it. I thought it was heresy to insult the mother ship. All you native Texans are pretty arrogant."

"We have reason to be…despite the heat," he added ruefully, replacing his hat and wanting desperately to wrap this up before he pounced on her.

"So I'm to believe that everything in Texas is bigger and better?"

Shock immobilized him. Was Bailey flirting with him? Surely not. He glanced over his shoulder at her. As far as he could tell, nothing in her demeanor was the least bit sexual. Too bad. "Yes," he said curtly. "I thought you would know that, being from Dallas."

"I'm not *from* Dallas. My dad was in the army. We lived all over the world. Dallas is where I'm assigned at the moment."

"So where do you call home?"

Seconds passed. Two, maybe three. For a brief moment he saw bleak regret in her brown-eyed gaze. "Not anywhere, really."

Such rootlessness was hard for him to imagine. Texas was as much a part of his lifeblood as breathing. Sensing her unease with the topic, he turned to face her, at last somewhat in control of himself. "Well," he said laconically, "at least if you weren't born here, you came as soon as you could."

Bailey, arms wrapped around her waist, smiled. "I guess you could say that."

He pursed his lips. "Apparently, I have no

choice about your interference. Is that what you're telling me?" The facts of the matter still stuck in his craw.

"You've got it." Though seeing him admit defeat must have pleased her, Bailey's expression remained neutral.

"Very well. Meet me at the club at ten in the morning. I'll show you where to get started."

"I'm a highly trained computer specialist, Gil. I shouldn't have to take up more than a week of your life."

Too bad. He glanced at his watch. "Come say goodbye to Cade."

In his office, he watched, perturbed, as once again his son lit up at seeing their visitor.

Gil's son beamed. "I unlocked three more levels, Bailey."

She nodded. "Good for you."

Cade looked at his dad. "Are you gonna call her *Bailey?*"

"I suppose I will," Gil admitted. "She's going to be around for a while."

Cade grinned charmingly. "That's good."

Gil pinched the boy's ear. "Behave, brat. I don't need your help finding women."

Bailey's face turned crimson, affording Gil a definite sense of satisfaction. It was fine by him if she felt uncomfortable. It was only fair. She was messing with his life from stem to stern in all sorts of ways. Not the least of which was his recalcitrant libido. The sooner she finished what she had to do and left town, the better.

Bailey arrived at the Texas Cattleman's Club fifteen minutes early the following morning. A heat wave still held the area in an unseasonable grip. Though by no means reaching the brutal temperatures of July and August, the day was plenty warm. Which meant that the winter clothing Bailey had brought with her was stifling.

Deciding she could maintain a professional demeanor *without* her blazer, she stripped it off and laid it carefully in the backseat of the car. Rolling up the sleeves of her white silk blouse, she breathed a sigh of relief as she immediately felt cooler.

In all honesty, part of her warmth stemmed from the prospect of facing Gil Addison again. Gil was in the clear as far as the investigation went, but she was going to have to work with him to some extent in order to do her job. The fact that she was attracted to him complicated things.

As she approached the club, she assessed the physical features automatically. Built around 1910, the large, rambling, single-story building was constructed of dark wood and stone with a tall slate roof. For over a century, it had been an entirely male enclave. In the past couple of years, however, a handful of women had finally been admitted as official members. During her stay in Royal, Bailey had heard rumblings of discontent. Not everyone thought change was a good idea.

Despite her early arrival, Gil was waiting for her in the lobby. Guests were admitted only in the company of a member. She wondered if Gil felt he was betraying his position by bringing Bailey into the mix.

She greeted him quietly and looked around. High ceilings gave a sense of spaciousness even as dark floors and big leather-upholstered furniture created a cozy, masculine space. "Nice," she said. "Is Cade with you?"

Gil pointed to the room just to the left of the entryway. "The old billiards room has been converted into the new day care center. I promised

Cade if he behaved nicely for a couple of hours, he could join us for lunch."

"I'd like that," she said. "Your son is a pretty awesome kid."

"I happen to think so." He shoved his hands in his back pockets. Today, perhaps in deference to his position as president, he wore a tweed blazer over a white dress shirt. He hadn't given up his jeans, however. Although Gil hadn't worn his hat inside his own home, apparently within the walls of the club, a Stetson was de rigueur.

It wasn't fair, Bailey thought desperately. How was she supposed to be businesslike when everything about him made her weak in the knees? Well, *almost* everything, she amended mentally. His arrogance was hard to take. She had come up against Gil's bullheadedness in her initial interview with him. Pushing for answers had been like a futile military assault against well-fortified defenses.

Gil was a man accustomed to steering his own course. Though she didn't pick up any vibes that he scoffed at the idea of a woman working in law enforcement, nevertheless she suspected he didn't like having to cooperate.

As they walked down the hall toward Gil's TCC office, she asked the question that she should have asked the day before. "Have you been to see Alex since he's been found?"

Gil pulled a key from his pocket and unlocked the solid oak door. Ushering Bailey inside, he nodded. "I did…but since he's lost his memory, the visit was rather pointless. He had no clue who I was."

"Were you close before he disappeared?"

"Close enough. Not bosom buddies, but we knew each other pretty well."

"You probably should go see him again when you have a chance," she said. "You never know when a face or voice might jog something loose."

"I'll think about it…."

She placed her purse and briefcase on a low table. She and Gil were standing in what appeared to be an outer reception area. More masculine leather furniture outfitted this small space. Someone had added a stuffy arrangement of artificial flowers, perhaps hoping to soften the ambience. But with various examples of taxidermy staring down from overhead, it was hard to imagine any woman feeling at home here.

Apparently, the office itself was through the closed door a few steps away. "I don't want to snarl up your day," she said. "If you don't mind writing down the user name and password…and giving me a quick rundown of the program you use to input information, I should be able to work on my own."

Gil smiled, genuine amusement on his face. That expression alone was enough to shock her. But the momentary appearance of an honest-to-God dimple in his tanned cheek took her aback. "Did I say something funny?"

He stepped past her to open the other door. "See for yourself."

Expecting to discover the customary computer and printer equipment inside, she drew up short at the sight facing her. A dozen wooden file cabinets, four drawers high, lined the opposite wall. By the window, a deep bookshelf housed a collection of thick leather ledgers. Dust motes danced in a sunbeam that played across a patterned linoleum floor. A battered rolltop desk sat just to the left, its only adornment a brass placard that said President.

She held up her hands in defeat. "You can't be serious."

Gil leaned in the doorway, his relaxed posture in direct opposition to her own state of mind. "There's something you need to understand, Bailey. The Texas Cattleman's Club is an institution, certainly as much a part of Royal's history as the churches and the mercantile or the feed store and the saloon. Men have come here for decades to get away from wives and girlfriends… to play poker and make business deals. Anyone who walks through the door as a full member has money and influence."

"And your point?"

"Heritage and tradition are etched into the walls. The guys around here don't like change."

"Which is why the child care center drew so much controversy."

"Yes. That, and the inclusion of women. So it shouldn't come as any surprise to see how we keep records. The good old boys may have their iPads and their internet, but when it comes to the TCC, the old ways are the only ways. At least so far."

"So there's hope for modernization?"

"Maybe. But I can't force it on them. It has to be a gradual process. If I'm lucky, and if I can spin it the right way, they'll think it was their idea to begin with."

"And it won't hurt matters if a few of the old guard ride off into the sunset in the meantime."

"You said it, not me. The TCC was here before I was born, and it will be here long after I'm gone. I'm under no illusions that being president gives me any real power. It's more of an honorary title, if you want to know the truth."

"I'm sure they think a great deal of you."

His eyebrows lifted. "Why, Ms. Collins. Was that a compliment?"

The teasing grin caught her off guard. Apparently, dumping her in a dusty room full of nothing but file folders sweetened his mood. "I doubt you need compliments of *any* kind, Mr. Addison. In fact, I'm surprised your head isn't already too big for that clichéd cowboy hat."

"Don't insult my hat," he said solemnly, though his eyes were dancing. "Since I'm stuck with you for the foreseeable future, we might as well drop the formality, don't you think?"

"Does that mean you trust me now?"

"Not for a minute," he said promptly. "But I figure it's my job to keep an eye on you...Bailey."

The way he said those two syllables made her stomach curl with something that felt a lot like desire. But such an emotion was doomed to wither on the vine. Despite her unwilling host's humor, she was not deceived. Her presence at the TCC was tolerated at best.

For a man who was innocent of any wrongdoing, Gil seemed curiously suspicious of authority. Was there something in his past that made him so? What did he have to fear from Bailey? Nothing that she could see. So perhaps it was government interference in general he hated. Not a particularly uncommon attitude, especially in this neck of the woods. But she felt the sting of his disapproval nevertheless.

Maybe in time she could prove to him that she was more than an outsider meddling in his business. She liked to think they could get to a place where he regarded her as something more than a nuisance. In a tiny corner of her heart, she wondered what it would be like if she and Gil were on the same side. If no walls between them existed. If they could be just a man and a woman. Exploring the sweet lure of attraction.

"I suppose I'd better get started," she said, trying not to let him see the way her hands trembled and her breathing quickened at the thought of actually being on friendly terms with the sexy rancher.

"Start where?"

"Are you genuinely interested, or is that another suspicious question?"

He shrugged, straightening and running a hand across the back of his neck. "A little of both, I guess."

She nodded, deciding not to take offense at his honesty. "My plan is to pull all the files of the people I interviewed in the initial investigation. I'll comb through them and see if anything stands out."

"In other words, you're looking for a needle in a haystack."

"Despite what television and movies would have you believe, law enforcement is seldom glamorous."

"Why did you choose this career path?" he asked, his gaze reflecting genuine interest.

Bailey hesitated.

"Sorry," he said quickly. "None of my business."

"No. It's okay. I suppose I was debating how to answer that. As a teenager I would have told you I wanted to serve my country."

"And that's not true?"

"It *is* true, but I'm not the starry-eyed idealist I was back then. And I'm a little more self-aware, I think. I've come to understand that I do what I do because I wanted to make my father proud of me."

"I'm sure he must be."

She grimaced. "Not really. He wanted me to go into the military. He's a career army guy. But that never seemed like the right fit for me, so state law enforcement was my compromise. I thought he would come around eventually, but he hasn't."

"Parents can be shortsighted. Do you regret your choice?"

No one had ever asked her that. Her job was fulfilling and she was good at it. But she wasn't sure it was going to be her life's work. "To be honest, I wanted to be a musician. I'm pretty good on the guitar and the piano. I took advantage of almost all my electives when I was in college to sign up for music courses."

Gil stared at her. Hard. As if trying to see inside her head. "You're an interesting person, Bailey Collins."

She might not be the most experienced woman on the planet, but she knew when a man wanted her. The look in Gil's eyes was unmistakable. There was enough fire and passion in his dark eyes to make her body go liquid with longing. She had felt the spark the first time they met and doggedly ignored it because he was a potential suspect.

But Gil was innocent, and the feelings were still there. If she encouraged his interest, things might get very intense during her time in Royal. The truth was, she was afraid that getting involved with someone who played a role in her investigation was unprofessional at best. Keeping a clear line between business and pleasure was not going to be easy.

She met his gaze reluctantly. "So are you, Gil. So are you."

He jerked when she said his name. As if her utterance of that single syllable shocked him. Now the frown returned in full force. "I have things to do," he said gruffly. "Are you all set?"

If she hadn't known better, she would have thought he was ready to beat a hasty retreat. "I'm fine," she said. "How long do I have before we meet Cade for lunch?"

"A couple of hours. He gets a snack at the center, so I made a reservation in the dining room for twelve-thirty. Does that work for you?"

"Of course. And will I be able to come back this afternoon and pick up where I left off?"

"Yes. Feel free to leave everything out. I'll lock the door when we go to eat, and no one will bother your papers."

"You're being very accommodating all of a sudden."

"I've been pretty rough on you," he admitted, his neutral gaze hard to read. "I know you're merely doing your job. I don't like it, but I suppose there's no point in shooting the messenger."

She took a step in his direction just as he did the same. Suddenly they were nose to nose in the small office. Her hands fluttered at her sides. "Thank you, Gil. Your cooperation makes my life a lot easier." She heard the huskiness in her voice and winced inwardly. Her eyes were level with his throat. They stood so close to each other she could see the hint of a dark beard on his firm, sculpted chin.

Without warning, Gil slid his hands beneath her hair, thumbs stroking her neck. He tipped her face up to his, their lips mere centimeters apart. His beautiful eyes teemed with turbulent emotion "You're going to be trouble, aren't you, Bailey Collins?"

"Why would you say that?" she asked, knowing full well what he meant but wanting to hear him admit that the attraction wasn't one-sided.

His lips brushed hers in a caress that could barely even be called a kiss. She leaned into him, wanting more.

But straight-arrow Gil Addison was a tough man. "Women and government are always trouble. When you put both in the same package, there's likely to be hell to pay."

Three

Bailey leaned against the desk for a full three minutes after Gil left the room, her legs like spaghetti. She had wanted to know if he had felt it, too, the heated connection between them. Now she had irrevocable proof. It was a wonder the tiny room full of aging paper hadn't gone up in flames on the spot.

Fanning her hot face with one hand, she reached for her briefcase and pulled out her laptop and portable scanner. It was one thing to contemplate seducing the steely-eyed rancher, but another entirely to realize that all he had to do was touch her and she melted.

She was here to do a job. Before she contemplated any hanky-panky, she needed to get her priorities in order. Fortunately, she had made a plan already, so even though her concentration was shot, she was able to follow through with her agenda.

The method of attack was fairly simple. Using a list of interviews from her earliest days in Royal, she pulled file folders methodically, keeping them in alphabetical order. Though she hadn't anticipated the complication of not having anything digitized, she would cope. As long as she didn't do something stupid like knocking a pile of paper off the desk, she should be able to proceed with relative efficiency.

Thirty minutes later she had finished reading through three folders and had developed a throbbing tension headache. She banged her fist against her forehead. Not only was much of the information *not* typed or organized in any discernible fashion, but the handwritten portions were barely legible.

To call this mess *record-keeping* was generous. It was impossible to compare one file with the next, because every member's information was different. Other than an initial sheet that documented simple details such as name, address and date of initial membership, all the other pages were a hodgepodge of business deals, sporting records and family connections.

It took her another half hour, but she finally managed to come up with a spreadsheet that allowed her to input the pertinent items that might be of use in the investigation. Her stomach growled more than once. She hadn't eaten breakfast, too nervous about meeting Gil again to be very interested in food.

She glanced at her watch and sighed. The minutes crawled by. Perhaps she was bored with the job, or maybe she was looking forward to lunch with Gil and his precocious son. Her distraction didn't bode well for the days ahead....

Gil prowled the familiar halls of the club, pausing again and again to greet and chat with men he had known for years, many of them since he was a child at his father's side. He was comfortable within these walls, centered, content. The Texas Cattleman's Club had suffered a few growing pains lately, but it would survive and thrive.

Tradition and stability were important. Which

was why Gil had passed the day-to-day running of his ranch over to other hands so he could concentrate on his son's well-being. One day, everything Gil owned would go to Cade. Cade would get married, settle down and hopefully have better luck in the romance department than his father had.

What really stuck in Gil's craw was the knowledge that the genesis of his unease sat not far away, her beautiful head bent over a stack of dull club papers, trying to find dirt on someone who might be Gil's friend. Perhaps the real problem wasn't that Gil didn't trust Bailey. Perhaps what bothered him the most was the notion that someone in Royal could have committed such a terrible crime.

Alex was back home, true. But a man with no memory was as vulnerable as a baby in the middle of a busy city street. How would Alex know if the perpetrators came at him again? How would anyone ever know what evil roamed the streets of Royal if Alex *never* remembered?

For years, Royal had been a great place to live, to raise a family. Occasionally the sheriff was forced to contend with cattle rustlers. And once in a while a two-bit drug dealer might try to set up shop. Of course, there were the usual domestic disturbances, or teenagers letting off steam on a Saturday night. But all in all, Royal was a pretty safe place.

At least it was until Alex Santiago had disappeared. The local and state authorities had crawled all over the town in the beginning. There were rumors of a potential drug war or maybe even bad blood between Alex and Chance McDaniel, who had appeared interested in the same woman. But since that time, everyone Gil knew intimately had been marked off the suspect list.

Which was all well and good except for the fact that *still* no one knew who the kidnappers were.

Maybe Gil should be more helpful to Bailey. He wanted his town back to normal, and Bailey wanted to close her case. So perhaps it was in Gil's best interest to help her. The sooner she was finished, the sooner she would leave town and go back to Dallas. That would be the smartest thing that could happen.

Gil didn't need the complication of an uncomfortable sexual attraction that was not likely to go anywhere. Already, Gil's son liked Bailey.

Which meant that soon Cade would be weaving scenarios where Bailey became his new mom. Gil had seen it happen before. The boy's unwavering fixation on finding a mother meant that Gil no longer dated in Royal.

Not that he ever had dated much. When his physical needs became too demanding, he either dealt with them via a cold shower, or he met up with an old female friend in another town who was as uninterested in a serious relationship as Gil was. Those encounters left him feeling empty and oddly restless. But Gil had yet to find a woman who came even close to what he thought his son needed.

Bailey was a career woman whose job involved a lot of travel. Though Bailey and Cade had clicked at their first meeting, Bailey didn't strike Gil as the nurturing type. Cade had lost so much. If and when Gil ever remarried, it would be to a woman with traditional values, a woman who believed in the importance of being a full-time parent.

Gil had played that role for a very long time. And never once regretted his decision. Cade's sweet spirit and outgoing personality were proof that Gil had at least done something right. But Cade would soon be going to school full time. As much as Gil would miss his son, he was looking forward to once again taking an active role in the management of the Straight Arrow.

What he and Cade needed was a down-to-earth woman, one who would supervise the domestic staff, plan meals for the housekeeper to carry out and organize social events…tasks Gil had no interest in at all.

That paragon of a woman was out there somewhere. Gil had to believe she was, because the prospect of spending his entire life as a single parent and a single man sounded very lonely indeed.

At ten after twelve, he gave up the pretense of being busy and headed back to his office. Bailey didn't appear to have moved at all since he left her two hours ago. She was surrounded by stacks of paper. Her fingers flew with impressive speed over the keys of her laptop computer.

She didn't even notice when he came in.

He cleared his throat. Bailey's head snapped up as she glared at him. "It wouldn't hurt you to knock," she said. "You scared me to death."

"It's *my* office," he responded mildly. "You're only visiting." He grabbed a ladder-back chair and turned it around, straddling the seat. Bailey was behind his desk, so he now faced her across the cluttered surface. Her thick russet hair was drawn back into a ponytail at the nape of her neck. Tendrils waved around her face. Her work must have been frustrating, because the vibe he was getting from her was definitely harried. "Problems, Bailey?"

Her eyes narrowed. "You *knew* how impossible this was going to be, didn't you?"

He lifted a shoulder. "I have the utmost faith in your capabilities." He paused. "Any luck?" He didn't really want to get involved in what he considered a breach of privacy for the members of the club, but at the same time, he didn't want to be blindsided with any surprises.

She gnawed her lip, her gaze flitting back to the computer screen. "It's a little early to tell. But I do have some questions about this man." She shoved a folder toward Gil. "According to his file, he's been cited three separate times for fighting on club property. Do you know if he had any kind of grudge against Alex Santiago?"

Gil glanced at the name on the tab and shook his head, grinning. "Just a good ole boy who gets rowdy when he's had one too many beers. We keep track of such incidents, just in case, but our policy is to prevent members from doing damage to themselves or anyone else. Someone usually takes the offender home and keeps his keys until the following day. I know this guy, Bailey. He didn't kidnap Alex."

The slight frown between her brows deepened. She handed him a second file. "And this one? He filed a formal complaint when the club hired a Hispanic chef. His letter includes a number of racial slurs."

Gil flipped open the folder and shook his head. "You're grasping at straws. There are bigots everywhere. But that doesn't mean this guy had any reason to kidnap Alex." He touched her hand briefly, surprising himself when he felt a *zing* of something from the simple contact. "Have you considered the possibility that you might be stirring up unnecessary trouble?"

"What do you mean?"

She was so earnest, so dedicated to her work. And clearly able to take care of herself. Even so,

Gil felt a distinct urge to protect her. Her white silk blouse was thin, thin enough for Gil to notice the outline of a lacy bra. Despite her extensive training and her credentials, she seemed vulnerable and surprisingly feminine even taking into consideration her deliberately bland and professional clothing.

Bailey's soft skin, gently rounded breasts, and graceful hands reminded Gil that beneath the outer shell of efficiency, she was a woman. He met her brown-eyed gaze with a calm he didn't feel. Some way, somehow, he had to convince her to back off this investigation. The feeling in his gut could be called premonition…or simply common sense. But he trusted that feeling…always.

"What you're doing is dangerous, Bailey. If word gets out that you're poking around in the TCC records, whoever kidnapped Alex may get spooked and try to harm you."

She sighed and closed her computer. "Is this genuine concern, or are you trying to get rid of me?"

"All of the above?" He asked it jokingly, but he sobered rapidly. "Alex escaped and made his way back home. Which means somebody out there is really pissed off and may try again. There's a good chance Alex is still in danger. By involving yourself in his situation, you court the same trouble."

Her chin lifted. "I'm doing my job. No more, no less."

"And if your job could get you killed?"

"I'm a paper pusher, Gil."

"You're a pain in the butt," he groused, realizing he wasn't going to win this round. But hearing her say his name was a small victory, nevertheless. He stood and held out his hand. "I'm starving, and Cade will be, too. Let's go find him."

The club dining room was packed. Bailey looked around with interest as the hostess led them across the floor. In a far corner at a table for two sat Rory and Shannon Fentress, still basking in the glow of being newlyweds. It was rumored that Rory had his eye on the governor's mansion.

Like Bailey, Shannon was not much of a girlie girl. She owned and managed a working ranch and dressed accordingly when she was in town on business. Judging by the way Rory looked at his new wife, he liked her just the way she was.

Gil had reserved a table by the window because Cade liked to watch the horses outside. Though of course the TCC had a parking lot, it wasn't at all unusual for someone to ride up, tie his mount to the wooden railings out front, and saunter inside for a bite of lunch.

Cade was his usually bubbly self. "I'm glad you're eating lunch with us, Miss Bailey." His form of address was the compromise Gil had allowed in his insistence that his son learn manners.

Bailey smiled at him. "Me, too. Did you enjoy yourself this morning?"

Cade nodded, already filling his mouth with crackers.

Without saying a word, Gil removed the basket from his son's reach. "I think a lot of the members have been surprised at how nice it is to be able to drop off a son or daughter or even a grandchild and to know that the kids are close by, happy and safe."

"Do you think the trouble is over?"

"I do. I really do. I still hear grumbling, of course. Particularly from the old guard."

"You mean like him?" Bailey cocked her head unobtrusively, not letting Cade see. A few tables away sat Paul Windsor, a charter member of the TCC.

Gil grimaced. "Yeah. He's one of the worst. But even so, I doubt he'd ever actually do anything to cause problems for the center."

Bailey shuddered inwardly. She had interviewed Paul during her initial investigation, and the man had given her the creeps. Divorced four times, Windsor considered himself a ladies' man. During the course of her questioning, Bailey had discovered without a doubt that Windsor was perhaps the most overt and obnoxious chauvinist she had ever met. He made no secret of his disdain for Bailey.

"I feel sorry for Cara," she said, "having such an overbearing father." Bailey knew what that was like far too well.

"I'll admit…Windsor can be a jerk. But he wields a lot of influence around here, so it would be a plus to stay on his good side if you want to make any progress with your investigation. If he were to raise a stink, he could convince others that you shouldn't be here in the club."

"But I have a legal warrant."

"Yes. And ultimately that would prevail. In the interim, though, things could get ugly."

"Is my presence going to cause big problems for you, Gil?" The thought troubled her.

He laughed, his dark eyes warm and teasing. "I can handle trouble, Bailey. Don't worry about me."

Cade, tired of being ignored, piped up, a sly smile on his face. "Do you know how to cook, Miss Bailey?"

Bailey raised her eyebrows. "Where did that come from?"

Cade took a bite of the hot dog their server had delivered moments ago. Pausing to chew and swallow, he fixed her with the blue eyes that helped make him such a cute kid. "I dunno," he said, the picture of innocence. "Dad says when I'm getting to know someone, it's nice to ask them questions…but not too personal," he added hastily, glancing at his father with a guilty expression.

"That's good advice," Bailey said. "So, in answer to your question, yes…I'm a pretty good cook. I started learning when I was not much bigger than you."

Cade nodded solemnly, his milk mustache adding to his charm. "And do you like little kids?"

Suddenly, she understood what was happening. She was being interviewed for a job. As Cade's mommy. *Dear Lord.* Fortunately for her peace of mind, the rest of their meal arrived, and in the hubbub of drink refills and the server's chatter, the moment passed.

Bailey had looked forward to an intimate lunch with the two Addison men, but unfortunately, this was not the venue. Gil could barely eat his meal because of repeated interruptions from club members happy to see him. What Bailey suddenly understood was that Gil had sacrificed an enormous amount in choosing intentionally to be the caregiver for his son.

Over the course of almost five years, Gil was wealthy enough to have hired the best nannies in the world. He could have gone about his business, running the ranch, hanging out at the TCC, meeting women, perhaps marrying again. Instead, he had made his son a priority. Fortunately, his current role as TCC president was more of an honorary position than a demanding job.

The enthusiasm with which club members greeted him during one short lunch indicated both that Gil was extremely popular and well-liked, and that he likely was not able to be present at the club as often as many of his cohorts.

Cade bore the intrusion of one table guest after another with equanimity. Several of the men addressed him personally. For a child not yet old enough for school, his composure and patience were commendable.

Not many boys of Bailey's acquaintance would be able to tolerate an extended meal in public without raising a ruckus. She sneaked him a couple of extra French fries off her plate while Gil was otherwise occupied. "Is it always like this?" she asked.

Cade nodded. "Yep. Everybody likes my dad." The words were matter-of-fact, but Bailey heard the pride behind them.

"So," she whispered conspiratorially, "do you think we get dessert?"

Cade wrinkled his nose. "If I eat most of my

salad." He stared dolefully at the small bowl, clearly not a fan of spinach mix.

"I remember once when I was about your age, my mother made me eat black-eyed peas that I didn't like. I broke out in a rash all over my whole body, and I never had to eat them again."

"Can you teach me how to do that?" Cade's eyes widened with fascination.

"Unfortunately, I think the rash happened because I was so upset. But you could always try using a red marker to put dots all over your skin. I'm kidding," she said hastily, suddenly visualizing an awful scenario where Gil realized Bailey had been giving his son tips on how to bypass healthy eating.

"I know that." Cade rolled his eyes. "You're funny, Miss Bailey."

Bailey had been called a lot of things in her life...responsible, hardworking, dedicated. But no one had ever called her funny. She kind of liked it. And she very much liked Gil's precious son.

Gil stood and touched Bailey's shoulder. "If you two would excuse me for a few moments, I need to speak to a gentleman at that table in the corner. I won't be long, I promise."

"Your food will get cold," Cade said.

"I bet the chef will warm it up for me. Love you, son. Back in a minute." Gil kissed the top of Cade's head and strode away.

Four

Bailey looked for signs that Cade was leery of being left with a virtual stranger, but quite the contrary. With his dad out of the picture, Cade was free to resume his interrogation. "What *kinds* of things do you like to cook?" he asked, returning to the original topic.

"Well, let's see…" Bailey folded her fancy napkin and laid it beside her plate. The meal had been amazing. Tender beef medallions, fluffy mashed potatoes and sautéed asparagus. A hearty meal that men would enjoy. Not a ladies' tearoom menu with tiny bowls of soup and miniature sandwiches.

She grinned as Cade poked halfheartedly at his

spinach. "I love to bake," she said. "So I suppose I'm good at bread and pies and cakes."

Her companion's eyes rounded. "Birthday cakes, too?"

"I suppose."

"My birthday is comin' up real soon, Miss Bailey. Do you think you could make me a birthday cake?"

She hesitated, positive she was negotiating some kind of hidden minefield. "I'll bet your dad wants to surprise you with a special cake."

Cade shook his head. "Our housekeeper will make it. But her cakes are awful and Dad says we can't hurt her feelings."

Just like that, Bailey fell in love with Cade Addison. How many years had she come home from school on her birthday, hoping against hope that her father had remembered to stop by the corner grocery and pick up a store-bought cake.

But he never did. Not once.

By the time she was nine, Bailey had quit expecting cakes. Two years later, she quit thinking about her birthday at all. It was just another day.

"I tell you what, Cade," she said, wondering if she were making a huge mistake. "If I'm still here when your birthday rolls around, and if your father doesn't mind, then yes…I'd be happy to make you a cake."

Cade whooped out loud and then clapped a hand over his mouth when several people turned around with curious looks. "Sorry," he mumbled.

"It's okay. This room is noisy anyway. Eat your salad, and when your dad gets back, we'll order dessert."

Cade managed four bites with some theatrical gagging, but when Bailey didn't react, he finished it all. "Done," he said triumphantly.

She high-fived him. "Now that wasn't so bad, was it?"

"I guess. But I'd rather have ice cream."

"Who wouldn't?"

They laughed together. She marveled at the connection she felt with this small, motherless child. On impulse, she leaned forward, lowering her voice, though it was doubtful she'd be overheard in the midst of the loud conversations all around them. Texas cowboys had a tendency to get heated when they discussed politics and religion and the price of feed. There was a lot of testosterone in this room.

"I want to tell you something, Cade."

He looked up at her trustingly. "Okay."

"I know you want a mother, but you are a very lucky little boy, because your dad loves you more than anything in the world. Do you know that?"

He seemed surprised she would ask. "Well, yeah. He tells me all the time."

"Not all dads are like that." Her throat closed up as unexpected emotion stung her eyes.

Cade stared at her, mute, as if sensing her struggle. "Are you talking about *your* daddy, Miss Bailey?"

She nodded, trying to swallow the lump. "My mom ran away and left us when I was about your age. And she never came back. So it was just me and my dad. But he wasn't like your father. He was…" She trailed off, not sure what adjective to use that an almost-five-year-old would understand.

Elbows on table, chin in hand, Cade surveyed her solemnly. "He was mean?"

Out of the mouths of babes. "Well, he didn't hurt me, if that's what you're thinking. But he didn't care about me. Not like your dad cares about you. Be patient, Cade. One day your father will find a woman he loves and he'll marry her and you'll have that mother you want. But in the meantime, be a kid, okay? And not a match-maker."

Gil halted suddenly, shock rendering him im-mobile. Bailey Collins had just given his son the kind of advice Cade needed to hear. And she had done it lovingly and in a way he could understand at his young age. Gil was torn between gratitude for her interference and compassion for the per-sonal pain she had revealed.

He backed up a step or two and approached the table again, this time more loudly. "You were right, Cade. I bet my lunch is cold. Sorry it took me so long. You ready for dessert?"

Bailey flushed from her throat to her hairline, her expression mortified. "How long have you been standing there?" she asked.

He kept his expression neutral. "I just walked across the room, Bailey. Why?"

"No reason," she mumbled, taking a gulp from her water glass.

Gil noticed the exchange of glances between his son and Bailey, a conspiratorial look that was oddly unsettling. Gil was accustomed to being his son's sounding board, his protector, his go-to guy. To see the boy so quickly accept and relate to Bailey made Gil worry. Perhaps he should keep the two of them apart.

When Bailey returned to Dallas, inevitably leaving a heartbroken Cade behind, Gil would have to pick up the pieces. On the other hand, would it be fair to deprive Cade of a relationship that provided him enjoyment in the meantime? Again, the frustration of being a single parent gave Gil heartburn. He was not the kind of man to unburden himself to anyone and everyone.

He had friends. Lots of them. But raising Cade couldn't be left up to a committee vote. Gil had to decide what was best for his son.

Over ice cream and pound cake, Cade grilled his father. "Are you and Miss Bailey going to do this every day?"

Gil lifted an eyebrow, looking to Bailey to answer that one.

"A week…ten days. I'm working as fast as I can, but it's slow going."

Cade grinned widely. "I like the child care center. They have a computer station and about a jillion Lego blocks, and my friends miss me when I don't come."

Gil rubbed a smear of ice cream from his son's chin. "Well, in that case, I'll set up some meetings with the executive committee for the next few days and get some club business out of the way."

When the meal was over they dropped off Cade and headed back to Gil's office. Walking in, he noticed the faint, pleasing scent of Bailey's perfume lingering in the air, something light and flowery. The scene that transpired in the dining room had affected him deeply. It was hard to mistrust a woman who treated his son with so much gentleness and compassion.

"Do you need any help?" he asked abruptly, wishing he had a reason to stay.

Bailey glanced at him, her gaze guarded. "No. But thanks."

He leaned a hip against his desk. "What do you do for fun, Bailey Collins?"

"Fun?" The question appeared to confuse her.

"I'm assuming you've heard of the word."

"I have fun," she said, her tone defensive.

"When?"

Her mouth opened and closed. "I like to read."

"So do I. In bed. At night. But what do you do in your leisure time?" He shouldn't have mentioned the word *bed*. His libido rushed ahead in the conversation and visualized the two of them entwined on soft sheets.

Bailey shrugged. "I work long hours. But in the evenings I like to walk around my neighborhood. It's a close-knit, established community with sidewalks and people who sit on front porches. I have several older friends I check on from time to time."

"Sounds nice."

"It is."

"And is there a man in your life?" Well, he'd done it now. There was no way she could interpret his question as anything other than what it was. He was attracted to her. And he wanted to know if he'd be stepping on any toes were he to follow up on those feelings.

Bailey glanced at her watch. "I need to get back to work."

"Does that mean, 'Back off, Gil'?"

"What? No. Not at all. But I…"

He waited. Silently.

"You don't even like me," she said, her expression troubled.

"Correction. I *tried* not to like you. That first day in the police station when you were grilling me like a seasoned pro, I found you wildly appealing, despite my disgruntlement. And since I am a man who believes in laying all the cards on the table, I think you should know."

"What changed?"

"Dogs and children are very good judges of character. My son adores you already."

"But that makes you uncomfortable."

The sadness lurking in her brown eyes shamed him. "It does. I don't want him to get too attached to you."

"Because I'll be leaving soon."

"Yes."

"I suppose I can understand that."

"It has nothing to do with you personally. But Cade has this unfortunate tendency to latch onto any woman who walks into my life, no matter how briefly."

"Why haven't you married again?"

He hadn't expected the blunt question. It caught him off guard, and for a moment, grief, regret and disappointment flooded his stomach. He shoved the negative feelings away. "There aren't too many women these days happy to be stuck out on a ranch in the middle of nowhere."

"Oh, please," Bailey said, giving him a reproving look. "You're rich, handsome and successful. I'm sure some poor soul in Royal would apply for the job."

Her mock scolding erased the momentary sting of allowing the past to intrude. "But not you?"

"I have a job."

"One that could get you killed." The realities of her position still disturbed him. Alex needed to get his memory back in a hurry. Before somebody else got hurt. Gil hadn't meant to change the subject, even if he was genuinely worried about her. "May I be honest with you, Bailey?"

"Please do."

"As angry as I was with you when we first met, I felt a definite *something*. In the weeks you've been here, I haven't stopped thinking about that feeling and wondering if it was one-sided."

She paled and wrapped her arms around her waist, clearly shocked by his candor. "It wasn't one-sided," she said quietly.

Exultation flooded his veins, despite the tiny voice inside his head that said he was making a mistake. "Good to know." The three words were gruff, but it was hard to speak when arousal made his entire body tense with need. "There's more," he said.

A tiny smile appeared and disappeared. "I'm bracing myself."

He stood up, no longer able to feign relaxation. "It's not easy for a single man my age to live in a place like Royal and do something as prosaic as dating. When Cade was almost three, I tried it for the first time."

"And?"

"It was terrible. Everyone tried to give me sympathy and child-rearing advice, or they offered to bake me casseroles."

"Not altogether bad things."

"Of course not, but I wanted to forget for a while that I was a single dad. I wanted companionship and…"

"Sex."

He saw no judgment in her gaze, but his cheeks reddened nevertheless. "Yeah," he sighed. "It would be easier if I lived in a big, anonymous city, but here in Royal everything I do is fodder for the gossip mill. I value my privacy, and I don't think my personal life needs to be front-page news."

"But you don't want to spend a lot of time out of town because of Cade."

"Exactly."

"You've given up a lot for him."

Gil frowned. "I haven't given up anything. He's my son. And I love him."

Bailey crossed the tiny distance between them. Putting a hand on his chest, she looked up at him. "You're a very nice man, Gil Addison." Her smile warmed him to a sobering degree.

He moved restlessly, fighting the urge to grab her. "It's not about being nice, damn it. It's what a parent does."

Some of the light left her eyes. "Not all of them."

He wanted to tell her that he had heard what she said to Cade, that his heart broke for a little girl with no mother and a surly dad. But her confidences had to be freely given or not at all. He wouldn't embarrass her that way. "Cade is the best thing that has ever happened to me. His childhood will pass quickly enough. I don't want to miss out on anything."

She went up on tiptoes and pressed a soft kiss on his lips. "If you're asking me to spend some… *time*…with you while I'm here, then the answer is yes. I understand the rules. You don't have to worry. And I will do my best not to let Cade get attached to me."

He winced. "God, you make me sound like an ass."

Her expression was wry. "Not at all. You're simply a straight arrow of a guy who doesn't hide behind platitudes. I respect that."

He gave in to temptation and stroked his thumb over her cheekbone. "You have the softest skin," he muttered. Slowly, he cupped her face in his palms and tipped her mouth toward his. "Have I told you how much your ugly suits turn me on?"

Bailey melted into him. "My suits are not ugly. They're professional." Her tongue mated lazily with his, hardening his sex to the point of pain. Of all the dumb ideas he'd ever had, this one ranked right up near the top. The door wasn't locked. Though no one was likely to disturb them, their current behavior was risky at best.

He kissed his way down her throat, toying with the buttons on her silky top. Bailey's eyes were closed, her lips parted. More than anything he wanted to bend her over his desk and take her hard and fast. Lust wrapped his brain in a red haze. His hands trembled as he found his way past her blouse to her breasts covered in lace.

Each soft mound was a full, perfect weight in his hand. He squeezed gently, shuddering when Bailey's low moan went straight to his gut and stoked the fire. He was rapidly reaching the point of no return. The problem with long bouts of celibacy was that a man tended to go a little insane when the woman he wanted was in touching distance.

"Tell me to stop," he pleaded.

Her hands tore at the lapels of his jacket. He helped her remove it and tossed it aside. He was burning up from the inside out.

"Touch my skin," she pleaded.

How could he say no? Each delicate nipple furled tightly as he stroked her with reverence. He lifted her onto the desk. Now he could reach her with his mouth. Shoving aside the gossamer cups of her bra, he first licked her, then suckled her, growing more and more hungry with every second that passed.

Her hands tangled in his hair, pulling him closer. "Bailey. Bailey…" He didn't even know what he wanted to say.

"Gil," her voice was little more than a whisper.

He inhaled sharply, close to begging. "What?"

"I think we have to stop. I don't want to, but we're at the club."

"At the club?" He could barely make sense of the words. He needed to be inside her more than he needed to breathe.

She shoved him, her two hands braced on his shoulders. "Stop, Gil. Please."

At last her protest penetrated the fog that bound him. He staggered backward, wiping his mouth with the back of his hand. It hurt to look at her. He leaned against the file cabinet, burying his face in his arm. Agony ripped through him. He had caged the tiger that was his lust for too long, and now the animal was free.

Seconds passed. Minutes. He sucked in great lungfuls of air, desperately trying to regain control. Behind him he heard rustling sounds as Bailey adjusted her clothing.

When her hand touched his back, he jerked. "Don't," he groaned. "Not if you want me to leave."

"I don't want you to go," she said quietly. "But for now, you have to. I'm sorry."

He whirled around. "Sorry for what?"

Her eyes were huge and dark. "I didn't mean for this to happen."

"Neither did I. At least not right now." He had never been as torn as he was at this moment. Everything inside him insisted he lock the door and make her his. But he dared not. Not for her sake, and not with his son in the same building. "We'll talk…tonight…when Cade is in bed. I'll call you and we'll make plans."

Her gaze searched his. "I'd like that very much."

Five

Gil didn't call that night. Bailey took his silence stoically, though deep inside her, a little kernel of excitement shriveled. Clearly, Gil's second thoughts about getting involved had trumped his momentary sexual need. She could understand his reluctance. He was not free to follow every whim or passing fancy.

In the cold light of reason, he had probably weighed the risks and benefits of getting involved with her and decided it was too risky. It hurt that he hadn't bothered to call and tell her straight up that he had changed his mind, but perhaps he'd been busy with Cade.

As much as it pained her to admit it, Gil's

about-face was probably for the best. Bailey had her own doubts. She'd never been a rule-breaker, and though it wasn't technically illegal or even unethical for her to have a personal relationship with Gil, it was at the very least unwise.

She needed to be able to rely on him as a source of information in her investigation. If he ended up in a position of having to defend one of his friends against her accusations, the situation could get ugly fast. No matter how much she responded to Gil physically, it was better for everyone if she ignored the needs of her body and her heart and focused on doing her job.

The following morning, she and Gil met at the club as they had the day before. Only this time, Gil still had Cade in tow. Not by word or expression did Gil evidence any memory of the heated interlude in his office the afternoon before. Bailey didn't know whether to be relieved or insulted, but she guessed he didn't want to give anything away in front of his son.

Cade bounced up and down in his father's grasp, finally breaking free long enough to wrap his arms around Bailey's thighs in an exuberant hug. "Hey, Miss Bailey," he said. "Are you going to eat lunch with us again?"

Bailey glanced at Gil. The slight negative shake of his head let her know the answer. "I'd love to, Cade, but today I'll probably just snack at my desk. I have a lot of work to do."

The disappointment in his big blue eyes filled her with guilt. "I understand." His body language imploded, leaving him long-faced and dejected.

Gil's jaw tightened. He removed a key from his pocket and handed it to Bailey. "I have a full schedule today," he said, the words terse. "Be sure to lock the door whenever you have to step out. I'll stop by before you go home and retrieve this."

"Thank you," she said, her words as stilted as his. As she watched, Gil turned on his heel and led his son toward the entrance to the child care center. Cade looked over his shoulder at Bailey just before they disappeared. She gave him a little wave and smiled, hoping to cheer him up. Truthfully, she liked the little boy, almost as much as she liked his taciturn father.

Feeling unsettled and confused, she made her way to the office and got to work. Today went a little faster, since she had at last decided how to comb through the files in a way that was more organized and less haphazard.

Here and there names popped out at her. Slowly, she began to build a list of men she would like to interview. She wondered if Gil would stonewall her when she suggested it. Every man she flagged had been interviewed in the initial investigation, but with Alex still in the dark, it was imperative that she not miss any links to motive or opportunity.

Her stomach growled loudly midday. Fortunately, she had an apple, a bottle of water and a granola bar in her tote bag. No one was allowed to eat in the club dining room unless he or she was the guest of a member. And since Gil had made it clear that he wasn't interested in sharing lunch with Bailey, she was on her own.

She could have taken a break and headed over to the Royal Diner. The food was good and the ambiance cheerful, but she wasn't in the mood to talk to anyone, much less defend her reasons for spending time at the club. Often, her job made her as popular as an IRS agent.

The day crawled by, but at five o'clock, she

was satisfied with the amount of work she had accomplished. She had shut down her laptop and was straightening the various stacks of files she was using when, after a brief knock, someone opened the door.

It wasn't too difficult to guess the intruder's identity. Bailey was very proud of her calm, friendly smile. "Hello, Gil. I was just finishing up." She fished in her pocket. "Here's the key."

When he took it from her, their fingers touched. His were warm and slightly calloused. She almost jerked her hand away in reaction, but instead, turned to scoop up her tote bag and purse. "See you tomorrow." If her voice had been any brighter, she could have powered a lightbulb.

Gil touched her, curling his hand around her forearm. "Stay," he muttered. "For a minute."

Her stomach quivered at the unmistakably intimate tone. But she wouldn't be so easily won over. "No."

"Please." His dark eyes were contrite.

"You didn't call me last night," she said evenly. "That was rude and uncalled-for."

He nodded. "I know. I'm sorry."

"Why didn't you?" She was genuinely curious in the midst of her pique. Gil was standing so close, she could see the tiny flecks of amber that gave light and depth to his night-dark irises.

He stroked her arm, almost absently, with one fingertip. "I couldn't decide what I wanted to say. You confuse me." His breath was warm on her cheek.

"Is that good or bad?" To hear that he was as conflicted as she was calmed some of her indignation. Today, he wore a simple button-down oxford shirt in lemon-yellow. The color suited him. As did the neatly creased dress slacks whose precision fit came only from hand-tailoring.

Bailey wished she had worn something more appealing than her usual workaday attire, but an investigative agent on the job had to be prepared for any eventuality. Occasionally, despite the clerical nature of her customary assignments, she had to chase down a bad guy or crouch in a grimy location to do surveillance.

Feminine vanity was useless in her line of work. Unless, like Sandra Bullock, she was ever called upon to pose in a beauty pageant, her chances for wearing seductive clothing on the job were slim.

Gil ignored her pointed question. But judging

from the way he looked at her, the answer was definitely *good*. "Have dinner with me tonight," he said abruptly. "Cade is spending the evening with my cousin and his wife. I don't have to pick him up until nine. I'll take you to Claire's."

Claire's was an upscale restaurant with white linen tablecloths and real silver cutlery, definitely a special-occasion place. Bailey's heart beat faster at the implications. And because it did, she was determined not to let him see that his invitation rattled her. "As long as I pay for my own meal to avoid any ethical considerations. And besides, are you sure you want to be seen with me in public?" Her tart question was a fair one given his ambivalence.

He winced. "I deserve that. I'll admit that I still don't like what you're up to…a witch hunt that may bring down one of my friends. But I find that my scruples are far less compelling than the taste of your lips."

Pulling her close, he kissed her gently, lazily. Where yesterday had been frantic and laced with desperation, this contact was infinitely sweet, deeply tender, endlessly erotic. She linked her arms around his neck, sighing when he aligned their bodies perfectly.

As a teenager, she had hated being taller than many of the boys in her class, but now, her height gave her an advantage. She felt the press of his belt buckle against her belly, inhaled the spicy scent of his aftershave. Beneath her fingertips, his hair was silky and smooth.

He held her confidently, like a man who knew his way around a woman's body. Despite his professed lack of opportunity, his technique was not rusty at all. Against her breast, she felt the steady thud of his heartbeat. Perhaps it was a bit ragged, who could tell? She only knew that this moment had been weeks in the making.

"You're very persuasive," she whispered. When his teeth nipped the ticklish spot below her ear, she laid her cheek on his chest.

"Is that a yes?"

"I'll have to go home and change. I could meet you back here in an hour." She was staying at McDaniel's Acres. Though she had no time to indulge in the dude ranch activities offered, her single room in the spacious ranch house was comfortable and more private than a B and B.

Gil tugged her ponytail. "I'll pick you up."

"It's not necessary."

He stepped back and cupped her face in his big hands. Searching eyes met her reluctant gaze and held it. For one instant, she felt a connection that was more than physical. "Don't fight me on this, honey," he said. "No matter how we both might twist and squirm in the wind, we're caught in this together. Let's see where it leads us."

"It won't lead anywhere," she said flatly, not sure why she had to remind him of that.

His half smile was laced with self-derision. "But we might have fun along the way, right?"

She wasn't armed against the charm of a man whose masculinity was as potent as hundred-proof whiskey. He had made an indelible impression on her the first time they met, and nothing had changed in that regard. "I suppose I have to wonder if you'll stand me up," she muttered. "Considering I waited by the phone last night like a silly schoolgirl."

With his thumb, he traced the curve of her ear, a newly discovered erogenous zone. "I'll make it up to you." Suddenly, he was kissing her again. Any sweetness that had lingered on their lips was instantly vaporized by a shot of pure fire. She felt it from her breasts to her pelvis, a tingling, sizzling vein of sensation.

His arm was hard across her back, his erection thrusting urgently against her lower body. The unapologetic passion he offered her was persuasive. She wanted to melt into him, feeling incredibly alive yet, at the same time, fearful of losing herself.

She pulled away, though it required great resolve. "I'm going now," she said, the words hushed.

Gil stood, head bowed, and pressed the heels of his hands against his eyes. "I'll be there at six-thirty. Don't make me wait."

He shuddered when the door closed behind her. Bailey had no idea how tenuous his control was around her. Perhaps she imagined that her drab clothing could disguise the appeal of her body, but she was wrong. When he held her, he felt the strength and softness of her frame. Neither skinny nor overweight, she was the epitome of a healthy young woman. Her required training regimen kept her fit. He liked that. A lot.

And though it only made his physical discomfort worse, he couldn't help imagining all that energy and flexibility at his disposal in bed. God help him.

When he could leave the room without embarrassing himself, he locked the office and went in search of his son.

Thirty minutes later he dropped Cade off in town and raced back out to the ranch to change clothes. Taking Bailey out tonight would spark gossip, but for once, he didn't care. Perhaps if word got around that the two of them were an item, no one would look too closely at Bailey's reasons for spending time at the club.

As he drove out toward Chance McDaniel's thriving operation, he contemplated the fact that Chance was about the only person he could think of who might have an ax to grind with Alex Santiago. Both men had shown interest in Cara Windsor, but it was Alex who had managed to put an engagement ring on her finger. Since Alex and Chance were very close friends, Chance might have seen the other man's actions as a betrayal of their friendship.

Gil wasn't sure what impact Alex's disappearance and subsequent memory loss had made on Alex's relationship with Cara, but it couldn't be easy for a woman to be with a man who didn't remember her.

As Gil pulled up in front of the impressive ranch house, Chance waved at him from across the corral. It occurred to him that Bailey must be seeing a lot of the handsome, blond cowboy. The lick of jealousy he felt was disconcerting. Chance was his friend. And since Bailey still had not ruled out Chance as a suspect, Alex was relatively sure that neither Bailey nor Chance would be inclined to get chummy. With Bailey suspicious and Chance on the defensive, they would likely keep their distance.

Gil's unsettling thoughts were derailed when Bailey stepped out onto the front porch. His first thought was "Hot damn." She had worn her hair loose, and it rippled around her shoulders in the evening breeze. Her gaze met his directly, but with a hint of reserve. She still wasn't sure of him.

The knowledge hurt. He'd been so busy with his self-righteous indignation at being questioned, he hadn't paused to consider how his truculence would affect Bailey.

He met her halfway up the stairs and held out his hand. "You look beautiful," he said, wishing there was another word for her vibrant appeal. The black knit, V-necked wrap dress she wore emphasized her narrow waist and curvy breasts. Cap sleeves revealed slender arms.

"Thank you."

Bailey's skirt ended several inches above her knees. For the first time since they met, Gil got a glimpse of her legs. The vision was enough to hog-tie his voice. He decided then and there that it was a crime for such beauty to be covered up by an ugly pantsuit. But on the other hand, at least her mode of dress meant other men weren't ogling her.

Gil considered himself an evolved, twenty-first-century kind of guy. Yet when it came to Bailey, he was finding himself strangled by impulses that were decidedly Neanderthal. He had no right to be possessive, no right at all. But he couldn't deny what he was feeling.

Conversation languished on the ride into town. By the time they were seated at Claire's and looking over the menu, though, he recovered enough to make small talk. "Have you eaten here before?" he asked.

Bailey shook her head with a grin. "No. These prices are a little bit above my per diem meal allowance. But I can splurge occasionally."

Gil chuckled. "I can recommend the salmon and the beef bourguignonne."

He barely noticed what he ate. Bailey was enchanting…sweetly serious about her job, and yet she possessed a dry sense of humor that took him off guard at times. He knew they were being watched by curious diners, most of whom knew him well. But he couldn't bring himself to care. It was the most enjoyable evening he had spent in a long, long time.

Over coffee and dessert, he decided he had to come clean about the secret he was holding. "Bailey…"

She smiled at him. "Yes?"

"I have a confession to make."

Some of the sparkle left her expression. "Oh?"

"I heard what you said to Cade. About your father."

Color flushed her cheeks and then faded away, leaving her pale. "I see."

"I'm sorry. I didn't want to embarrass you yesterday."

"But it's okay tonight?" The words had a bite to them.

He shrugged. "I need to have honesty between us. It's important to me. You don't have to explain, but I *am* sorry that your childhood was so difficult. I really appreciate what you said to Cade. It was very generous of you."

She crossed her arms, the posture unconsciously defensive. "I had food and shelter growing up. Lots of kids don't have that much."

"True. But love is important. Perhaps your father didn't know how to show you what was in his heart."

"I told myself that when I was a teenager. I took a psychology class in high school. Learned a little bit about how pain can make people turn inward. But it didn't really help to know the reason why. My father and I barely speak. A couple of awkward meals at the holidays. The obligatory birthday gifts. I tried for years to get him to open up to me, but he's a stone wall with no apparent desire to change."

"He's missing out," Gil said soberly.

Bailey exhaled and took a drink of water, her hand trembling visibly. "Thank you."

After a moment's awkward silence, she leaned forward and clasped her hands on the table. Her beautiful brown eyes were earnest. "If there's a possibility that you and I are going to become… *intimate*…I wonder if I may ask you a personal question."

"Of course."

"Does Cade remember his mother at all?"

He hesitated. This wasn't a road he had expected to go down. But since he had inadvertently overheard Bailey's extremely personal confession to Cade, it seemed only fair that Gil should reciprocate. "No," he said slowly. "She died before his first birthday. Took her own life." Even now, it hurt to say the words. And since Bailey had dossiers on half the people in town, she probably already knew that.

"Oh, Gil. I am so sorry." Bailey took one of his hands in her two smaller ones and held it tightly.

He squeezed her fingers, warmed by her genuine sympathy. "It was a long time ago. And to be honest, our marriage was doomed from the beginning, though I didn't realize it for a long time. My wife had severe emotional problems that she hid well."

"You don't have to explain," Bailey said, still holding his hand.

"It's okay. I want to tell you. It might help you understand why I'm so protective of Cade. When things started to go wrong in my marriage, I urged Sherrie to go with me to counseling. In the safety of that situation she was able to reveal that she had been abused as a young teenager. I found it almost impossible to believe at first, but her parents were part of a religious cult that 'married' young girls in the church to older men."

Bailey released him and sat back, her gaze stricken. "That's horrible."

"Yes. To her credit, Sherrie really did want a child, and she was so happy to be pregnant. But postpartum depression took a toll on her, and she was never able to recover."

"So you made Cade your priority."

"Don't paint me as noble," he said soberly. "There was more to it than that. My in-laws took me to court and tried to steal Cade away from me. Faced with the prospect of losing him, I realized how much I loved that little innocent baby."

"Thank God they didn't succeed."

"I went through a hellish eight months of court-ordered visits and psychological evaluations…"

She nibbled her lower lip, her eyes huge, her expression sober. "I'm beginning to see why you have a chip on your shoulder about government intervention."

"I suppose I do, but I came close to losing everything. My in-laws paid off a judge, and it nearly worked. Fortunately for me, I have a lot of friends in Royal and in the state at large. Powerful friends. In the end, justice prevailed, but it was a close call."

"I've admired you since I first came to Royal," Bailey said quietly. "Now, even more."

Six

Bailey was shaken by what she had heard. Imagining Gil without his son was a picture she didn't want to paint. The two of them were a tight family unit. Despite the absence of a female figure.

She had wondered from time to time if Gil were still in love with his dead wife…and if that was why he hadn't remarried. Apparently, the truth was more complex. He wanted to protect his son, and that included not letting Cade's little heart get broken time and again if his father indulged in short-lived relationships.

Bailey had to admire Gil's selflessness. But how long could a virile, healthy man suppress his sexual needs before he did something reckless? Like initiating an intimate relationship with a woman he barely knew…a woman just passing through.

Sitting across the table from him was like a romantic fantasy come to life. She seldom had opportunities for fine dining, and never with someone who looked like Gil. His expensive black suit showcased broad shoulders and a trim waist. A crisp white shirt and red tie completed the image of a successful businessman. Though he would have fit right in wearing tooled leather boots, he had chosen more traditional dress shoes for their date. She found that she missed his cowboy look, though this man was wildly appealing, as well.

But no matter how much she was drawn to him, the truth of their situation gave her pause. If she made unwise choices and things blew up in her face, she could face a formal reprimand from her boss, or even worse. She'd seen other colleagues terminated because they let their judgment be clouded by personal involvement on a case.

Beyond the professional implications, Bailey didn't want to be Gil's guilty pleasure. She didn't want to be filed under the category *secret dalli-*

ance or *enjoyable mistake.* Not that he was hiding anything tonight. They were eating dinner in front of half the town, it seemed. But letting Cade know was another story.

Her suppositions were confirmed when Gil glanced at his watch and muttered in dismay. "It's almost time for me to pick up Cade," he said. "I didn't know it was so late. I'll run you home and come back to get him."

She and Gil had talked easily and at length, with a comfort that Bailey rarely found in relationships with the opposite sex. The time had flown by. Underlying all of the conversation was the unspoken subtext of what they both wanted.

"That's not necessary," she said. "Too much driving back and forth. Let me call Chance. I'm sure he won't mind sending one of the ranch hands into town to pick me up. Go get your son, Gil. Take him home to bed." The Straight Arrow and McDaniel's Acres, both south of town, were not that far apart. It made no sense for Gil to crisscross the county when the solution was simple.

Gil waved a hand for the checks and tucked both of their credit cards in the folio, frowning. "I invited you to dinner tonight. I'll take you home." He grimaced, clearly conflicted. "I suppose he's old enough to know that not every relationship ends in wedding bells. We might as well go get him together."

"I appreciate your chivalry," she said wryly. "But I don't need a grand gesture. I've already told you how I feel. You're a sexy, appealing man, and I find myself very attracted to you. That won't change simply because you have responsibilities."

The tightness in his jaw eased, and his expression lightened. "Thank you, Bailey." He stood and took her wrist to pull her to her feet. "But we'll go together."

Outside, the weather had taken a turn for the worse, or at least toward the more seasonable. Temperatures had dropped while they were eating, and now, wind-driven spritzes of raindrops dampened the air.

Bailey shivered, wishing she had remembered to bring a wrap. Gil shrugged out of his jacket and tucked it around her shoulders without asking. The fabric smelled like warm male. "Thank you," she said, drawing the lapels closer together.

The car was not far, so they made a run for it. Gil tucked her inside and ran around to the driver's seat. When they were both safely inside, they laughed, shaking water droplets from their hair. The windows fogged up almost immediately.

He didn't start the engine. Instead, he turned toward her and studied her intently. Her taut nipples pressed against the fabric of her dress, perhaps visible even through her thin bra. Not that Gil could see. But *she* knew.

"Do you need the heater?" he asked gruffly, his gaze dark and hungry.

She shook her head. "It's not that cold in the car."

Their stilted, prosaic conversation might have been funny if she hadn't been wound so tightly. Her skin hummed with the need to feel his touch. Fortunately for her, Gil must have been on the same page.

"Come here, Bailey." They were sitting in the front of his fancy, enormous truck. The wide bench seat presented all sorts of intriguing possibilities.

She scooted closer, barely noticing when his

jacket slipped away. "Why?" she asked. "Do I need to warm you up?"

His lips quirked in what might have been a grin had he not been so focused on finding her mouth with his. "Any warmer," he groaned, "and I'll be in danger of getting arrested." He cupped the back of her neck in one big hand and used the other to anchor her chin. Lazily, with no apparent hurry, he kissed her. His lips were firm and warm and took without asking. He tasted faintly of coffee and whipped cream.

"Gil…" The word trailed off on a whimper when he released her chin and found her knee.

Slowly, he glided his palm up her thigh. His whole body jerked when he discovered the edge of her stocking and the tiny satin rosette that was her garter. "Sweet heaven," he groaned. "You little tease."

She nipped his chin with sharp teeth. "I spend a lot of time on the job," she murmured, loosening his tie and unbuttoning two buttons at his throat. "When I dress up, I like feminine lingerie."

His fingers played with the edge of the stocking, his hand warm and hard. "Promise me something," he groaned, the words like ground glass.

She felt him trembling and understood the power she wielded. Both exultant and abashed, she struggled to find footing in the quicksand at her feet. Was this right for her? For Gil? What were they doing?

"Promise you what?" she asked. More than anything she wanted to take his hand and push it higher. But they were in a public parking lot, and it was time to pick up Cade.

"Promise me you'll wear this the first time we're together." He caressed the bare skin around her garter with his fingertip. Everything inside her went hot and shaky. She felt reckless, and that was enough to slow her down. Bailey Collins was never reckless. Not in her job and not in her personal life.

Someone had to be strong in the midst of insanity. This time it had to be her. With great regret, she removed his hand and slid to her side of the vehicle as far as she could go. "Will there be a time like that?" she asked.

"God, I hope so," he said, banging his fist on the steering wheel. "Because if I don't have you soon, I can't be held responsible for what happens."

He was exaggerating. She knew that. But the

desperation in his voice was real and unmistakable "Look at your watch," she pleaded. "We have to go."

That he obeyed her was no victory. She wanted to stay with him in the intimate confines of the truck cab. In fact, she would have stayed there all night if he had asked. Though she hadn't fooled around like that as a high school kid, the idea held a certain appeal to a woman whose love life had been barren of late.

On the brief drive to Gil's cousin's house, silence reigned. The swish of the windshield wipers was the only sound. At their destination, Gil parked by the curb and hopped out. Minutes later, he returned, carrying a sleeping Cade. At Gil's motion, she leaned across the seat and opened his door.

Gently, his face unreadable, he scooted Cade to the middle and belted him into his booster seat. The boy's body was limp. When he slumped in Bailey's direction, she put her left arm around him and held him close. He smelled like peanut butter and little-boy sweat.

Gil climbed in and stared at his son. "He's dead to the world."

"Just as well," Bailey said. "Maybe this will all seem like a dream to him."

"Thank you for understanding. Most women would be offended."

"Not me. You're a father first and foremost. I respect that. Cade is a very lucky boy." She kissed the top of the child's head. "Take me home, Gil."

Gil drove more slowly than usual, fully aware that he was distracted. Bailey's care and consideration for his son impacted Gil in ways he couldn't explain. His brain ran in circles, torn between imagining intimacy with Bailey one second and wondering how he could ever test a relationship with a woman without dragging his son into it.

At McDaniel's Acres he pulled to a stop in front of the ranch house and put the truck in Park. Bailey put a hand on his arm. "Don't get out. You can't leave him here alone."

Gil shook his head. "He's fine." He went around the truck and opened Bailey's door, holding her hand to help her out. Remembering what she was wearing beneath that demure black dress made him hard all over again. "Good night, Bailey."

He slid his hands beneath her thick, silky hair and anchored her head for his kiss.

She leaned into him, her lips eager and soft, her breasts crushed against his chest. Though he knew her to be tough and capable, when he held her like this, he wanted to protect her at all costs. The danger inherent in her job was never far from his mind.

He wedged a thigh between her legs, pulling her hips against his, letting her feel the extent of his need. "I'm working on an idea," he said. "Will you trust me?"

She toyed with his belt buckle. "Of course." The breathless note in her voice told him all he needed to know. He wasn't in this alone.

"Tomorrow. At the club. I'll explain."

"Yes." She ran her hand over the late-day stubble on his chin. He opened his mouth and bit gently on one of her fingertips.

The erotic action was a big mistake. The rush of lust almost crippled him. Backing away from her the way he would an angry rattler, he put the body of the truck between them. It was good that his son was asleep in the cab of the truck. Otherwise, Gil just might have taken Bailey standing up.

His forehead broke out in a cold sweat thinking about it. "Sleep well," he said, knowing that he wouldn't.

Bailey walked halfway up the steps, then turned to look at him. "I had fun tonight." Her voice carried on the night breeze. "Good night, Gil."

He got into the truck and leaned his forehead against the steering wheel, his heart slugging in his chest as if he'd run a marathon. Something was going to have to change. And soon....

Bailey entered the house quietly, though since it was not yet ten, likely no one was asleep. Chance McDaniel stood in the lobby chatting with a couple of gray-headed ladies from Ohio. Bailey had met them when she first arrived. Learning to ride a horse was a big item on their bucket list, and Chance's patient staff was helping that dream come true.

The owner of the dude ranch excused himself when he saw her enter and crossed the floor. "Everything okay?"

Her face must have reflected some of her turmoil. She flushed. "Fine. No problem."

He lifted an eyebrow. "Was that Gil Addison's truck I saw out front?"

Her flush deepened. "It was. We had dinner together."

Chance's smile was more of a grimace. "I suppose that means at least one of us is no longer on your suspect list."

"A man is innocent until proven guilty," she said.

Chance shook his head, his gaze hooded. "Doesn't feel that way from where I'm standing."

Bailey headed for the stairs, wishing she had the luxury of becoming friends with Chance. Already, in the short time she had been around, she felt like he was a man who could be trusted. But hard evidence was composed of facts and not feelings. Until she could completely clear his name from the suspect list, she couldn't get too friendly. It was impossible to imagine Chance committing a kidnapping. But she knew better than most that some people hid unimaginable secrets. Chance didn't. She was almost positive. Hopefully, soon she could prove it.

Upstairs, she stripped out of the one nice dress she had brought with her to Royal and stared at her reflection in the mirror. The tiny undies and demibra that matched the garter belt were intensely feminine. Closing her eyes, she tried to imagine the look on Gil's face if he saw her like this. His raw passion elated her, made her feel special and wanted.

In the shower, she imagined Gil at her side, his face all planes and angles as he stared at her with male determination. His body was intensely masculine, strong and rugged. The juxtaposition of his tenderness with Cade and his ruthless pursuit of Bailey should have confused her, but in a way, it made perfect sense. He was a man of deep emotions, whether it be love for his son or hunger for the woman in his arms.

She wouldn't be the woman in his *life*, not long-term. But if the fates were kind, she would certainly enjoy exploring her sensual side with him until it was time for her to leave.

Sliding her soapy fingers over her slick breasts, she inhaled sharply as arousal pumped through her veins like thick honey. Her nipples were taut nubs, their ache an ever-present reminder that she was young and in need of a man's touch.

Dragging the washcloth between her legs, she winced as her body demanded attention. It didn't take more than a few languid strokes before she came with a low moan and rested her forehead against the tile as her heartbeat slowly returned to normal.

On shaky legs, she got out and dried off, already anticipating the following day. What did Gil have in mind? And how long would they have to wait?

She was almost asleep when the cell phone on the bedside table vibrated suddenly. Snatching it up, she glanced at the screen. Though she had only dialed it once before, she recognized Gil's number. "Hello."

"Bailey. I just looked at the clock. I'm sorry. Were you asleep?"

"Not quite." She shifted, sitting up against the headboard. "Is something wrong?"

The silence on the other end of the phone lengthened. "Define wrong."

"Is Cade okay?"

Gil's voice was hoarse. "He's fine. Never even woke up when I carried him to his bed."

"That's good."

"Yeah." The awkward conversation was going nowhere. "I wish our evening could have lasted longer," he said.

She knew exactly what he meant. "Me, too." Suddenly, something struck her. "Are *you* in bed?" she asked, not sure if she wanted to know or not.

"Yes. And wishing you were here beside me."

She swallowed hard. The man was nothing if not honest. "I need you to be sure, Gil. Things will be complicated, and I don't want you to resent me when this is all over."

"I wasn't very nice to you at first, was I? And you're not sure if I fully trust you."

She heard the regret in his voice. "You were entitled to your opinion. In your place, I might have been just as aggravated. It's never easy to be questioned about a crime. It makes innocent people jittery. I understand."

"I don't want you to think I'm taking advantage of you. I really like you, Bailey. In spite of your job."

She smiled, smoothing her free hand over the soft, faded pattern of the double wedding ring quilt on her bed. "I like you, too, Gil. In spite of your bullheadedness."

"Touché."

His chuckle warmed her. "I'm not having phone sex with you," she said firmly, yet willing to be persuaded.

"Trust me, Bailey, when we finally have sex, it's going to be a helluva lot more exciting than mere words. I'm going to let you turn my world upside down and then return the favor."

Her breath caught as her legs moved restlessly against the sheets. "You're awfully confident."

"It has nothing to do with confidence. You and I are two of a kind. We're loners. Who feel things deeply and have a strong sense of responsibility toward those who depend on us. I think that's why I felt something for you the first day we met. You're not only beautiful and sexy, but you care about things. About people. About a little boy who wants a mother…."

"You know I'm not applying for that job, right?"

"I know. But how do you feel about the boy's father?"

Bailey sucked in a breath. Perhaps it was easier to be honest when he wasn't staring at her face to face. "I want to spend time with you, Gil…in all sorts of ways…."

He said something short and sharp that she couldn't quite hear. And then his voice echoed over the connection more strongly. "Not all women are as honest as you," he said.

She smiled, knowing he couldn't see. "Have I shocked you?"

"Only in the best possible way." He paused. "Go to sleep, Bailey. I'll see you tomorrow."

"Tomorrow…"

She fell asleep thinking about all the possibilities tied up in that one wonderful word.

Seven

Bailey worked her way through one drawer after another, her pile of file folders growing along with her list of questions. She'd been at the club all day, and Gil had never once shown his face. When she had arrived at ten as usual that morning, the club receptionist met her and handed over a key, saying that Mr. Addison had been detained.

Bailey tried not to brood over hurt feelings, but her reaction to Gil's absence was beginning to make her question whether it was wise to get involved with him at all. She didn't want to analyze his every move for evidence of whether or not he really cared. Fear of making an embarrassing misstep in their relationship kept her on edge.

At a quarter to five she began packing up her things, prepared to go home and pore over the new information she had gleaned. Still, nothing and no one jumped out at her as a likely suspect. But there were a lot of club members who had connections to Alex, and Bailey was pretty sure that given the chance to talk to them she might be able to make progress with her case.

When Gil walked into the small office, again without announcing his presence beforehand, she sucked in a sharp breath, but otherwise managed to face him with a neutral expression. Her hands continued to move, tidying up the work space, but her body was rigid.

Gil didn't look any happier than she felt. "I had five phone calls today," he said abruptly. "All of them wondering why I've allowed a woman I'm dating to spend time at the club without me present."

She winced. "So they know what I'm doing?"

"Not specifically. It's my fault for giving the receptionist my key. She's a nice woman, but she can't keep her mouth shut."

"What did you tell them?"

"I thought about making up a story, but frankly, you're a state investigator. Everyone in town knows it. Sooner or later, people were going to put two and two together. It was one thing for you to be seen eating lunch with Cade and me at the club. But I should have thought through the implications of you being here on your own today."

"So you told them the truth."

He nodded his head. "I did. And I can't repeat most of what was said in return. People don't like knowing that their personal business is being opened up to an outsider, especially one with government connections."

"I'm sorry, Gil."

"It's not your fault." He shrugged, his expression rueful. "You're merely doing your job. I can handle a little heat, Bailey. It's you I'm worried about."

"I told you…I can take care of myself."

"Alex Santiago would have told me the same thing, and look what happened to him. Some nutcase decided to kidnap him."

"There had to be a reason. Some connection we're not seeing."

"Yes. And because we can't point to the per-petrator yet, the danger is still very real. What if someone tries to dissuade you from probing any further?"

"I take precautions. That's one reason I'm not staying in town. Chance's place is as safe as any-where I can think of. Too many people around for anyone to get to me unnoticed. Not to men-tion the fact that I can keep an eye on Chance."

Gil ran a hand across the back of his neck, his face a thundercloud. "He has nothing to hide, Bailey. I'll be damn glad when this is all over."

"Not me," she said quietly. "At least not entirely. Because that means I'll have to head home."

His jaw tightened as the truth of her words sank in. Whatever time the two of them shared was likely to be very brief. Her heart shied away from that knowledge. Leaving Royal was a reality she didn't want to contemplate. Especially not now that Gil had admitted he wanted her.

He frowned as he took her shoulders in his hands and squeezed gently. "*Please* be careful, Bailey."

She moved closer into his embrace, kissed his cheek, and sighed. "I'm always careful." For long seconds, they stood there quietly as something fragile and precious bloomed. To have the right to lean on him, even symbolically, was very sweet. His hard frame seemed to shelter hers, even though she was quite capable of caring for herself.

The pull of his masculinity called to a part of her she often kept out of sight. Being "girlie" was the last thing she needed in her line of work. But with Gil, she felt herself letting down barriers. Softening. Needing.

"Tell me," she said, idly running her fingers over his collarbone. "What is this idea you were working on?"

He set her at arm's length, his expression unreadable. "You want to interview club members—right?"

"Yes. Maybe half a dozen or more."

"The thing is, Bailey, I can't stop you from doing what you were sent here to do, but I also can't condone using the club for those interviews. The TCC is where guys come to get away from life. To chill out and kick back. They have a right to their privacy. But…"

"But what?"

"But I think it might go down better if we do it at my place. I'll contact whomever you tell me and invite them out to the Straight Arrow tomorrow night. I won't lie. I'll tell them flat out why they're coming. But I'll throw some steaks on the grill and open a case of beer, and hopefully, we can mitigate any negative backlash."

"You'd do that for me?" What he was suggesting made perfect sense. Neutral territory.

He kissed her nose. "It's not that big a deal. But, yes."

"What about Cade? Will he be there?"

"Actually…"

For the first time since she had known him, Gil looked uncomfortable.

"What? What are you not telling me?"

"I have friends in Midland with a little boy exactly Cade's age. They're planning a sleepover birthday for their son and they want Cade to come. I'm driving him up there in the morning."

She fidgeted, not sure if she was reading him correctly.

Gil's smile was crooked. "I hope you'll pack a bag and stay at the Straight Arrow with me once our guests are gone."

* * *

Twenty-four hours later, Bailey drove out the familiar road to Gil's sprawling ranch, wondering how she had gone from being a hardworking investigator to a woman contemplating a night with her lover in one dizzying swoop.

The juxtaposition of professional and personal in the upcoming evening made her skittish. It was important that she come across as business-like and competent when she interviewed Gil's friends and acquaintances. If any of them got wind of what Gil had planned for later, her credibility would be shot.

But there was no real cause for alarm. Gil didn't want gossip any more than Bailey did. For his son's sake, if nothing else.

When she arrived, Gil greeted her at the door. Two high-end pickup trucks were already parked out front. "Come on in," he said. "I thought you could go ahead and get started before dinner. We'll set you up in the front parlor. It was always my mom's holy of holies, but I think it will give you the privacy you need."

As they traversed the narrow hallway to the back of the house, Gil suddenly dragged her to a halt and pushed her against the antique wallpaper for a hard, hungry kiss. "I missed you today," he muttered, his hips anchoring her to the unyielding surface.

She returned the kiss eagerly, inhaling the scent of starched cotton and well-oiled leather. Gil was dressed casually in jeans, cowboy boots and a white shirt with the sleeves rolled up. He radiated tough masculinity, and despite her advanced degrees and the level to which she had risen in her career, it was humbling and embarrassing to admit that she was definitely turned on by his macho swagger.

"I missed you, too," she said primly. "And I want you to know how much I appreciate all you've done to set this up tonight."

He nibbled the side of her neck. "You can thank me later. There's a full moon tonight. The view from my bedroom window is spectacular."

The breath caught in her throat as he hit a particularly sensitive spot. "Promises, promises..." She swallowed back an embarrassing moan. "There are vehicles out front. I assume we're not alone?"

As a protest, it was weak.

Gil rested his forehead against hers, his thumbs brushing the thin cotton of her blouse where it glided over her breasts. "You make me want to forget everything. That's dangerous."

"Should I apologize?" Her arms linked around his neck, feeling his warmth, his solidness.

"Come on," he said gruffly. "Let's get this over with."

Gil had to hand it to Bailey. She knew how to be charming. Her manner with the men he had invited hit just the right note. Neither authoritative nor tentative, she invited the guests to speak with her in private one by one. And as each man returned from the parlor, no one seemed particularly bent out of shape by Bailey's informal interrogation.

Over dinner, Gil surveyed the assorted group of men. Only two on his list had begged off. Sheriff Nathan Battle, who was on duty, and Paul Windsor, who was out of town on a business trip.

The rest had varying degrees of history with Alex Santiago. Douglas Firestone, Ryan Grant, the twins—Josh and Sam Gordon, Zach Lassiter, and Beau Hacket. With the possible exception of

Hacket, Gil liked and respected every man present. And even Hacket, despite his son's recent vandalism of the child care center at the club, hardly seemed the type to kidnap anybody.

Fortunately, the medium-rare steaks were a big hit, the beer held out, and Bailey had the good sense to excuse herself from the table before the party became rowdy. By the time the evening wound down around ten, Gil was fairly certain that none of his guests really remembered why they had come. Each one went home with his belly full and perhaps a forbidden cigar or two smoked on the way out.

Gil closed and locked the front door, leaning against it with a sigh. As male bonding went, the evening was a home run.

But all he could think about was getting Bailey naked.

He found her in the parlor, her laptop open, her head bent studiously over a legal pad of notes. "Did you get anything good?" he asked, sprawling in a chair that was more comfortable than it looked.

She glanced up at him, her teeth worrying her bottom lip. "I have no idea. They all claim to like

Alex. Firestone does admit to arguing with him, but insists it was nothing significant. Hacket tried to schmooze me and pretend that he's a saint. But overall, I came up with nothing that I didn't already know or suspect."

He saw the frustration on her face. "I invited Chance, but he was reluctant to come."

"I know. He glares at me when he thinks I'm not looking." She rubbed her temples with her index fingers. "I've had plenty of opportunity to talk to him, and if he's the kind of man to commit a felony, I'll be very surprised."

"Men in love do strange things."

"Is he? In love, I mean? You know him better than I do."

"I don't know. He and Cara were very close. But once Alex came on the scene, she had eyes for nobody else."

"So with Alex gone, Chance might try to make his move?"

"Even if he does, it still doesn't mean he had anything to do with Alex's disappearance."

"True…"

She stood up and stretched her arms toward

the ceiling. "Enough of this. I'm officially off the clock until tomorrow."

Gil linked his hands behind his head. "I like the sound of that."

Hands on hips, she stared at him.

"What?" he asked, raising an eyebrow.

"Will I seem hopelessly inexperienced if I tell you I'm nervous?"

He rolled to his feet and walked toward her, grinning when she backed up and nearly toppled an antique glass pitcher. "There's nothing to be nervous about."

"That's what you think. I'm having trouble with the shift from work to play."

He tucked her hair behind her ears, glad that she had left it loose tonight. "I can help with that." Scooping her into his arms, he ignored her squeak of protest. "We're alone at last. I thought they would never leave." Striding out of the room and up the stairs, he felt his heart beating faster and faster, though carrying his burden was no strain. "In case it matters," he said, nuzzling her ear, "you're the first woman I've ever invited for a sleepover."

* * *

Bailey clung to Gil's neck, mortified that he had picked her up. She was not a petite woman, yet he seemed completely at ease. In the midst of being flustered by his romantic gesture, she was also taken aback by the casual way he told her this night was special.

In the doorway to his bedroom, he paused. "Last chance to say no." His dark eyes held not a flicker of humor.

She ran her thumb along his chiseled jawline. "I don't want to say no. I need you, Gil. I want you. Even if this night is all we have."

His slight frown told her he didn't like that last bit, but she was trying to be practical. Cade couldn't be shuttled off to friends and neighbors all the time, and Gil didn't want to parade his love life in front of his son. Any way you looked at it, tonight's encounter was not likely to be repeated.

Gil strode toward the bed and set her on her feet. He held her hands, his expression unreadable. "I've watched you for weeks," he murmured. "And even when I told myself you were an officious pain in the ass, I knew in my heart that I wanted you."

"All I saw was the disapproval," she confessed. "It hurt that you thought so little of me. And you seemed angry all the time."

"A defense," he said simply. "I hoped you would leave and I could forget the way your hair shines with fire in the sunlight or the way your long legs carry you across a crowded street."

Bailey's heart fluttered. Poetry from the man who was pragmatic and straightforward. He didn't dress it up or spout it effusively, thus making the quiet, sincere words all the more powerful.

She swallowed. "I had no idea."

"You weren't supposed to. I've done my damnedest to stay away from you. But when you called me about access to the club, I knew I was a goner." His smile was lopsided. "A man can only have so much self-control, and you tested mine to the limit. Turns out, I'm not as strong as I thought."

"I wish I could tell you I'm sorry about that, but I'm not. I've had an embarrassing crush on you since we first met."

"Nice to know." He grinned, the flash of white teeth literally taking her breath away. Gil bore great responsibilities and had a serious streak a mile wide. But this man, this lighthearted, teasing man, looked younger and happier than she had ever seen him.

She tugged her hands free and punched him in the arm. "You have to know that every woman in town thinks you're a hottie."

His smile faded, replaced by a searing look in his deep brown eyes that made her toes curl. "The only woman whose opinion interests me is you, Bailey." He curled an arm around her waist and dragged her closer. "But I think I'm done talking."

Wild elation streaked through her veins. His arms were hard and strong, binding her without mercy. She kissed him recklessly, clumsily, as if somewhere a clock counted down the seconds they could be together. The air in the room was charged.

"Take off your boots," she demanded. Her fuddled brain knew the priceless antique quilt on Gil's bed shouldn't be damaged. He released her only long enough to obey, toeing off each one and facing her in his sock feet.

He should have looked more vulnerable, less of a threat. But somehow that wasn't the case. "Any other orders?" he asked, the words mild despite his hot, determined expression.

She nodded slowly. "Now the belt."

Like the boots, the belt was constructed of expensive hand-tooled leather. Gil unfastened the buckle and made a production of sliding the length of cowhide through each loop. When it was free, he coiled it and tossed it on a chair. His jaw flexed. His chest rose and fell rapidly with each labored breath. "Whatever you want, Bailey."

The way he looked at her made her body go lax with arousal, even as her hands fisted helplessly at her sides. Her thighs pressed together. Where her body prepared for his, she was damp and ready. She had known sexual desire in the past, but never this writhing hunger that turned her insides into an ache that consumed her.

Paralyzed suddenly by the knowledge that she wasn't really a femme fatale, she fell silent.

Gil seemed to read her hesitation. "You were on a roll," he muttered. "Don't stop now."

Apparently her bent for bossiness entertained him. She shifted from one foot to the other, realizing suddenly that her clothes were far too tight, much too hot. "The shirt," she said. "Unbutton it slowly."

Eight

She had created a monster. Straitlaced Gil Addison showed a definite talent for stripping. If he had loosened his shirt buttons any more slowly, Bailey might have lost it and ripped the fabric apart with her two hands. But she had asked and he had answered, so all she could do was watch as he tormented her.

When the shirt hung open, he stopped. She hadn't requested that he take it off, and he was obeying the letter of the law. His silence rattled her. What was he thinking? The uncertainty dried up any further desire to script this encounter. Her momentary lead in the dance no longer appealed.

They were separated by a distance of only three or four feet. Close enough for her to see the shadow of late-day stubble on his chin. The evidence of his masculinity underlined the differences between them. Bailey knew how to use a weapon and could even bring most men down using her training in martial arts.

Many people would describe her as tough.

But Gil…Gil was the real deal. His sleek, long-limbed body rippled with muscle. His olive skin gleamed with health and vigor. He was a man capable of defending those he loved. At the peak of his physical strength and power.

Bailey's heart twisted. Hard. What would it be like to be loved by Gil Addison? Clearly, he had loved his dead wife once upon a time. And of course he loved his parents and his son. But to be a woman loved by a man like Gil…that would be an incredible thing. In the present context, though, that thought was a fantasy, one she might as well put out of her mind.

Tonight was about human need. Sex. That was all. She and Gil were drawn to each other, because they both spent too many nights alone. So during this brief moment in time, they were

going to cling to each other and enjoy the plea-
sures of carnal excess.

Perhaps Gil was more intuitive than she realized, for he abandoned his sexy pose and stalked
her, backing her up until her hips hit the bed.
"You aren't saying much," he taunted. "Cat got
your tongue?"

She curled an arm around the bedpost, clinging
in hopes that her shaky legs wouldn't give out.
"Just admiring the view." It wouldn't do to let
him know how much seeing his beautiful body
in the privacy of his bedroom rattled her.

He shrugged out of the shirt and let it fall. Taking her free hand, he placed it flat over his heart.
"Feel what you do to me."

The rapid thud of his heartbeat was unmistakable. Without thinking, she rubbed gently, as
though she could absorb his life force through
her fingertips. Touching him was both intimate
and arousing.

Gil groaned and closed his eyes. Was it possible
that he was as turned on as she was? Experimen-
tally, she scraped her thumbnail across one flat,
brown nipple. Gil put his hand over hers, trapping it against his hot skin. "Don't poke the tiger,

Bailey. I have plans for tonight, and they don't involve coming too soon like a callow teenager."

His blunt speaking made her cheeks flame. "I want to please you. I need to know what you like."

"You *do* please me, in every way. I love your strength and your integrity. And I love the way you treat my son."

"He's lucky to have a dad like you."

Gil caressed her cheek, his gaze hooded. "I spend much of my time being Cade's father. I know that role inside and out. Tonight…" He paused and she saw the muscles in his throat contract. "Tonight I'm just a man. A man who wants *you*."

She slipped her arms around his neck, appreciating the distinction, even if it wasn't wholly true. Gil could have any woman he wanted, but in a town like Royal, such a relationship would be tricky. Sleeping with Bailey was less complicated. She understood that.

Resting her head on his shoulder, she whispered the bare, honest truth. "I want you to make love to me Gil. More than I've ever wanted another man. Don't make us wait any longer."

* * *

Gil felt the sting of strong emotion in his throat and his eyes. Bailey Collins was the most fascinating, unconsciously sensual woman he had ever met. Now that she was here—in his bedroom, about to make a number of his more torrid fantasies come to life—all he could think about was how soon he was going to lose her.

He slammed the door on those images. Who and what he needed was right in front of him… literally. Bailey was warm and real and so very, very beautiful. Running his hands though her hair, he imagined what it was going to look like spread across his pillow. "In other circumstances, I might insist that anticipation is half of the pleasure. But tonight, I'm in no mood to delay anything at all." He unfolded her arms from around his neck. "My turn, lovely Bailey."

As her cheeks turned the color of a ripe tomato, he undressed her bit by bit, supporting her arm as she stepped out of her clothes. His surmise had been right on target. She wore naughty undies beneath, this time pale pink trimmed in mocha lace. The tiny bikini panties and matching bra were ultrafeminine, reminding him that despite the toughness she exhibited in her job, Bailey was all woman.

She seemed reluctant to dispense with the final layer that shielded her full nudity. So he matter-of-factly shucked his jeans and boxers and socks in a couple of quick moves. Bailey's eyes widened. The expression on her face was gratifying.

He was fully erect, and aching to possess her. But first he was going to have to coax her into relaxing. "I don't know what you're thinking," he complained. "Is that deer-in-the-headlights look you're giving me because you've changed your mind or because I'm going too fast?"

She licked her lips, arms crossed beneath her breasts. "Neither," she said quietly. "I'm enjoying the moment."

"Could you possibly enjoy the moment under the covers? I'm getting cold feet."

That made her giggle, and some of the rigidity left her posture. "I'm on board with that."

He tugged her close for a quick kiss and then turned back the covers on the large, wide bed. His sheets were soft white cotton, scented with sunshine. The housekeeper was a big fan of using a clothesline, and truth be told, Gil liked it. The smell made him think of being a kid.

When he helped Bailey crawl beneath the sheet and the quilt, however, childhood was the last thing on his mind. His brain blanked for a moment, all his senses absorbing the novel and gratifying sensation of feeling Bailey's arms and legs tangle with his. She was soft, so soft. He held her tightly, burying his face in her hair.

"I've imagined this moment for weeks," he admitted, flattening his palm on her belly and teasing her navel with his pinkie. It would almost have been enough just to hold her. To revel in the knowledge that she had come to him of her own free will and *wanted* to share his bed.

Bailey kissed his chin, her hands roving across his pecs and his shoulders. "Does it measure up?"

He wedged a thigh between hers and groaned as his thick, almost painful shaft rubbed against her leg. "I'm not sure. I'm having trouble believing this is real. I don't want to wake up in a minute and find out I was dreaming."

Without warning, her hand closed around his erection. "I'm real," she said. "We're real. Here. Together."

When she began stroking him, his eyes closed involuntarily. He had been leaning over her on one elbow, but now he fell back on the bed, his hands fisting in the sheet. *Holy hell.* It wasn't the effects of extended abstinence making him insane. It was the way she touched him. Her gentle movements were exactly right.

The first sexual encounter between a man and a woman was supposed to be fraught with pitfalls, neither partner knowing the other's preferences. Bailey was putting paid to that idea. Everything she did was gut-level perfect. Now she was the one leaning over *him*, her silky hair falling around them as she kissed him softly. Kiss/stroke. Kiss/stroke. The sequence made him dizzy with lust.

His sex quivered every time her lips found his. He held the back of her neck to deepen the kiss and to make sure she didn't stop what she was doing. But soon, far too soon, he had to call a halt. Sucking in raw lungfuls of air, he shook his head, half-crazed with hunger. "Enough," he croaked. He hovered on a knife-edge of arousal.

As he predicted, the moon had found its way into his bedroom, the silver orb framed by his window. The drapes were open. Shafts of white light spilled over Bailey's face, giving her the look of an ice queen. But no ice queen ever emanated the kind of warmth that could save a man's life. Gil hadn't fully understood the depths of his loneliness until he brought Bailey to his home and to his bed.

He had told himself repeatedly over the past few years that being Cade's father was more important than anything. And it was. A sacred obligation. But Gil was neither a monk nor a saint, and in this instant he realized how sterile he had allowed his life to become.

Every cell in his body cried out at the indulgence of touching Bailey, of kissing her. Like flowers blooming wildly in the once-barren desert after a storm, he found himself drunk with pleasure. She rolled with him in the bed, laughing softly as they bumped noses.

"This is nice," she said, the voice more prim than her actions. "I never knew Gil-the-sex-maniac existed."

"You're not naked," he complained.

Sitting up, she reached behind her back and unfastened her bra, dropping it at the foot of the bed. Now, the moon painted two perfect breasts with a magical palette of light and shadow. Bailey dragged her hair over one shoulder, her head cocked as she tried to read his expression. He, unlike his partner, was cast in semi-gloom.

"Is this what you had in mind?"

"Getting there," he muttered. He slid his hand between her smooth thighs and stroked the center of her panties. The scent of her came to him, warm and heady. "These, too." Rising to his knees, he shoved the offending scrap of nylon down her hips.

Bailey lay back, arms above her head, and let him finish the job. The moon took her natural beauty and made it supernatural, as though a fairy or a sprite had come to him in a mirage. Touching her was the only way to prove she wouldn't fade away.

Kneeling between her legs, he leaned forward and mapped her body like a blind man, his caresses making her whimper and stir restlessly. Her face, her throat. Each lovely breast. The narrow span of her waist. The flare of her hips.

He stopped there, breathing hard. Running through the back of his mind was the knowledge that he was missing something very important, something key to this moment.

Bailey put a hand on his thigh. "Do you have condoms?" she asked softly.

He sensed that the question embarrassed her. "Yes." Leaving her momentarily was unthinkable, but he would never do something she would regret. After sheathing himself in latex, he went back to her, his hands shaking as he sprawled on his side.

She turned her head to look at him, her lips curved in a smile that made him want to drag her beneath him like a caveman. But his evolved side held sway…barely. Tonight was about more than his sexual starvation. It was about pleasing Bailey.

He parted her sex with gentle fingers and tested her readiness. Warmth and wetness met his touch. Inserting two fingers into her tight passage, he played with her until she began to beg.

"Now, Gil. Please. Now."

Surprisingly, her urgency enabled him to chain his own impatience. Though his arousal pulsed and throbbed like a raw, aching nerve, he found himself entranced with tormenting Bailey. Locating the tiny nub that was her nerve center, he rubbed softly, exulting when she cried out and arched her back as the climax rolled over her.

When she was limp and still, he began all over again.

Bailey didn't know what she had done in a previous life to deserve such a night of enchantment, but she wasn't about to complain. Her world had narrowed to the confines of Gil Addison's bed. Nothing beyond that perimeter mattered for the next few hours.

Her body sated with pleasure, she struggled to focus her fuzzy thought processes. She was aware that Gil watched her, hawk-like, his features masked in the semidarkness. His back was to the window, so while *he* could look his fill of her nakedness painted in lunar glow, she was less able to gauge his mood.

She lifted a hand and let it fall. "You've destroyed me," she said, the words slurred. Her orgasm had been intense, unprecedented. To realize that he could draw such a response from her was daunting. What if tonight's affair ruined her for other men?

When he touched her again, she flinched.

Laughing softly, he spread her legs and positioned the head of his sex at her core. "I want you to remember every second of this night," he said hoarsely. "Because I'm going to make love to you until neither of us can remember our names."

Bailey believed him implicitly. Heat radiated from his big body, warming her chilled skin. Now that her pulse had settled back to normal, the room was cool.

Gently he stroked her swollen folds with his shaft. She was so sensitized that the caress was almost too much. Incredibly, as he brushed her intimately, her body began to thrum again with the need for him, the urgency to have him inside her.

Suddenly, desperately, she wanted to turn on a light. She wanted to catch every moment of the insanity, to revel in every nuance of expression that crossed his face as he pleasured both of them.

Her breath caught when he cupped her bottom and canted her hips. "Now," he promised, the single syllable guttural. "Now, Bailey."

He was thick and hard. Her flesh yielded to his

penetration slowly. On the heels of her earlier climax, this claiming was overwhelming. She shook her head from side to side, incredulous that such feelings were real. Nothing in her past had prepared her for Gil.

He held her tenderly as he took her with the confidence of a man who knew what he wanted. What she wanted. Kisses interspersed with raw lunges that took him all the way to the mouth of her womb. His arms quivered as he kept his weight from crushing her into the bed.

She wrapped her legs around his waist, feeling the power, the potency. Her fingernails dug into his shoulders, marking him as hers. She could fall in love with him so easily... For many weeks she had watched him from afar, seeing the respect people afforded him, witnessing the joy in his son's face, understanding the position and influence Gil wielded in the community.

Tonight, though, her feelings went far beyond admiration. Gil had taken her heart. Perhaps he didn't even know it. Perhaps it didn't even matter. For a stolen moment in time the only real measure was how they each gave and received pleasure.

She clung to him as he thrust wildly, his force shaking the bed. A tendril of heat curled in her lower abdomen, spread throughout her pelvis and burst into full flame as she pitched over a sharp edge in the midst of Gil's hoarse shout of completion.

They must have dozed in the aftermath. When she opened her eyes, the moon had shifted and was barely visible in the corner of the window. The room was quiet. Gil lay half on top of her, his face buried in the sheet. Despite the chill in the air, they were both sticky with sweat.

She eased to one side, wincing when he muttered in his sleep. Stealthily, she moved an inch at a time until she could free herself and slide from the bed. After using the bathroom and freshening up, she pondered the possibility of a hot shower. The lure was impossible to resist. A thick terry-cloth robe hung on the back of the door, so she dropped it on the floor in arms' reach and turned on the water.

Soon, steam filled the roomy enclosure. Clearly, Gil had spent money on modernization at some point. Bailey applauded his choice. The bold turquoise and amber tiles reminded her of Spain's artistic influence in Texas architecture.

The water was hot and reviving, chasing the chill from her bones. She didn't bother with her hair, keeping it mostly dry. Though Gil had invited her to spend the night, she was already feeling anxious about "the morning after." Perhaps it would be better to say farewell and head on home very soon. Things that seemed perfectly natural and normal under the hypnotic effects of moonlight could develop into awkward realities in the cold light of day. She didn't want to spoil a perfect memory with an uncomfortable goodbye that left her feeling empty and lonelier than when she started.

Suddenly, the frosted-glass shower door opened and Gil's big body appeared in the opening. "Room for one more?"

Nine

Gil caught the play of emotions that skittered across his lover's face. Surprised pleasure. Shy embarrassment. Wary uncertainty.

She nodded. "Of course."

There was no *of course* about any of this. He and Bailey were breaking new ground, and he sensed that she had gotten cold feet in more ways than one. Giving her a moment to adjust to his presence, he took the soap and turned his back as he washed himself. His sex was hard and ready, but he wouldn't rush her. This was too important.

When he felt two hands on his back, rubbing his soap-slicked skin, he closed his eyes and smiled. "That feels good," he groaned, resting

his head against the wall, feeling the hot, stinging spray pound his skin.

Bailey's arms encircled his waist from behind.
He sucked in a sharp breath when he felt the press
of her soft breasts on his back. "I was thinking
about going home now," she said.

Gil jerked in shock and spun to face her, nearly
depositing both of them on the slippery floor. He
grabbed her upper arms to steady her. "What the
hell are you talking about?"

Her eyes were huge. She shrugged helplessly.
"You have employees and obligations. Tomorrow
morning things will be different."

"Different, how?" His temper simmered.

"You know…weird."

He ran a finger down her nose and shook his
head with a sigh. "Why do women have to be so
complicated?" He turned off the water and pulled
her into his arms, deliberately pressing his erection against the notch where her legs met.

"Life is complicated. *I'm* pretty simple."

He felt her shiver. "As much as I'd like to de-
bate that last point, I think I need to warm you
up. Put on my robe and I'll build a fire."

As they both dried off, he tried not to look at

her, but it was like telling sailors not to gaze at sirens on the rocks. His gaze tracked her every graceful movement. The moment when she shrouded her nude form in his enveloping robe was a major disappointment.

The fireplace in his bedroom was original to the house and, like the other three scattered throughout his home, cost a fortune to insure. He rarely took the time to use this one, because many nights he was late coming to bed.

Now, though, he was glad of the ambience.

In his peripheral vision he was aware of Bailey climbing back into bed and huddling under the covers. In addition to growing up on a ranch, Gil had been a Boy Scout, so he soon had a roaring blaze that popped and crackled and began to fill the room with cozy warmth.

He rose from a squatting position and found her watching him, unmistakable arousal in her eyes. Her lips parted. Her breath came quickly. Men were rarely as modest as women, so it gave him not a second's pause to stride toward the bed, naked and determined. She couldn't hide what she was feeling. Not now.

When he scooted in beside her, she squawked

as his cold feet made contact with her legs. He dragged her close, spooning her and kissing the nape of her neck. "I'm not letting you leave, Bailey. So get that out of your head. If you're worried about waking up tomorrow morning, perhaps I'll keep you up all night so it won't be an issue." He shuddered as he thought of the possibilities. "I don't have a problem with that."

She laughed softly, wriggling onto her side so she could face him. "You don't lack confidence, do you?" Reaching out, she ran her thumb over his bottom lip. Which seemed to Gil like an open invitation to nibble the tip of her finger. He sucked it into his mouth and felt the pull in his groin.

Breathing hard as he pulled back, he brushed aside the lapel of the robe she wore, baring her breasts. "It's not confidence if it's a fact. Every time I get near you, I get hard."

"Gil!"

He nuzzled her nose. "What, Bailey?"

She shook her head, surveying him with a slight smile. "I never knew you could be this way."

"I'm guessing you saw me as an uptight, judgmental, obstructive pain in the ass."

The smile broadened. "You said it, not me. But that's not all. I knew you were a gorgeous man and a loving father, so that balanced out your less stellar qualities."

"I'm sorry I made your job difficult."

"You're hardly the first. I'm rarely a popular person."

"I can't believe that. Criminals probably line up for the opportunity to be alone with you in a tiny interrogation room."

"You've been watching too many cop shows on television. I do a lot behind the scenes, but it's rarely glamorous."

He stroked her hair from her forehead, tucking it behind her ear. "I'm glad you're here tonight," he said, deadly serious.

Her gaze searched his. "Me, too."

This time, he was clearheaded, but no less hungry. He retrieved protection, rolled it on, and returned to her side. Slowly, wanting to draw out the moment, he moved over her and into her. Bailey lifted her hips and took him deep, her wide-eyed gaze holding mysteries he was unable to fathom. Did she feel the earth move? Was she already thinking about leaving him tomorrow?

The warm, tight clasp of her flesh on his made him woozy. He closed his eyes, concentrating on the lazy slide in and out. Bailey tried to urge him on with incoherent pleas. But he was set on a course that was as immovable and inexorable as the tides. What had started out as something of a one-night stand was shifting and changing. His brain shied away from the implications, even as he grappled with his need for her.

He had a son to consider. And a home in Royal. But the woman beneath him, her body soft and yet strong, had bewitched him. How could he go on with life as usual, knowing what he was giving up?

She was no happy homemaker in apron and pearls. Bailey was a competent career woman. Based in Dallas. Where she would have ample opportunities for advancement.

His body said with finality that the time for analysis was over. His jaw tightened and his legs quivered as the urge to come struck furiously and without quarter. Dimly, he heard Bailey cry out as she found completion. His own climax was more of a tornado, snatching him up, ass over heels, and dropping him into a void of sated bliss so dark and deep he wanted to revel in it forever.

They stayed in bed this time, too exhausted to move. Bailey's head lay on his chest. One of her arms curled across his waist. He floated on a sea of contentment that was unprecedented. In that moment, he believed anything was possible.

Bailey stroked his chest idly, her fingers tracing the line of hair that ran from his collarbone to his groin. So mellow was he that her first quiet question didn't even cause him heartburn.

She sighed softly, her eyes shielded by long lashes. "Will you tell me more about your wife?"

He kissed her forehead. "Not much left to tell. We married young. She had serious emotional problems. Her parents were wackos who subjected her to an unimaginable adolescence."

"Does Cade ask about her?"

"He used to, from time to time. Now he's more interested in finding Mrs. Addison Number Two."

"Has he ever visited his maternal grandparents?"

Gil stiffened. "Not a chance in hell. My wife took an overdose of pills but lingered long enough to beg me not to ever let our son near her parents or their way of life. The custody case drew statewide attention. I think the cult—for lack of a better word—that my in-laws embraced began to worry that the government might take a closer look at them, so they moved the entire group over the border into Mexico."

"I'm so sorry, Gil. It must have been a nightmare for you."

"It was a long time ago."

She was quiet for a few minutes, and then she sat up in the bed. "If you have one more of those little packets, I think I'm in the mood to see the view from the top."

When Bailey awoke the next morning, the spot beside her was empty. In an instant, full recollection of what she had done rolled over her in a mix of exhilaration and panic. Raising up on her elbows, she saw a note on Gil's pillow written in dark scrawl on a scrap of paper:

Didn't want things to be "weird," so I'm giving you your space.

He had signed his name and added a crooked smiley face. She smiled, half-sorry he wasn't with her, but more than a little relieved to have a moment to compose herself. Lying in Gil's bed felt deliciously decadent. She was usually an early riser, eager to start the day. But for once, she allowed herself a few minutes to revel in the memories of last night.

Becoming Gil's lover had been eye-opening. Never had she dreamed that inside his no-nonsense exterior was a tiger ready to pounce. He had wooed her, coaxed her, seduced her. And she had been a willing participant every step of the way.

The scent of his skin still clung to her pillowcase. When her body reacted to the images that masculine fragrance evoked, she knew it was time to get up.

After a quick shower, she dried her hair and dressed in the clean clothes she had packed in her overnight case. She made the bed, repacked her things, and carried the bag with her downstairs to set it by the front door. Coming face-to-face with the housekeeper was a bit of a shock, but the older woman never batted an eyelash. She smiled kindly and offered to scramble some eggs or make whatever Bailey wanted for breakfast.

Settling for black coffee seemed the safest

choice. Bailey's stomach fluttered with nerves. Even now, dressed and in control somewhat, the prospect of seeing Gil was nerve-racking. He was a contained man, a private man, and though he had opened up to her last night in a very intimate way, she did not delude herself into thinking that she knew him well. They hadn't been together long enough for that.

The housekeeper seemed flustered that Gil's guest wasn't interested in eating, so to keep the peace, Bailey accepted a plate of toast and carried it and her coffee out onto the back porch. The morning was chilly, but her blazer, the one at which Gil turned up his nose, was warm enough to warrant an alfresco meal.

It was a shock to find that her host had entertained the same idea. He sat on a cushioned wicker love seat, his phone and iPad on the glass-topped table beside him. When Bailey stepped out on the porch, he jumped to his feet. "Join me," he said, his smile warm.

She would rather have chosen the chair across from him, but that didn't seem to be an option. Her stomach tightened as she sat down at Gil's urging, hip to hip with the man who had wakened her twice during the night for lovemaking. Despite her best efforts, her cheeks reddened.

He rested an arm across the back of the seat, his fingers stroking her shoulder lightly. "Did you sleep well?" His voice was a low rumble, the words husky and intimate.

She set the plate of toast, uneaten, on the table, and gulped her coffee, not caring that it scalded her tongue. "Yes." Staring out across Gil's beautiful ranch, she pretended an intense interest in the view.

His fingers moved to her neck, just below her ear. "You're shy," he accused, humor in his tone.

The innocent caress turned her insides into a soft, yearning puddle of need, reminding her of the danger she faced. She was no more willing than any other woman to have her heart broken. "I'm thirty-three years old. I'm not shy."

"Then what is it? Look at me, Bailey."

She half turned, studying the face that had become dear to her. His chiseled good looks added up to so much more than a handsome man. His integrity, his decency, his willingness to do the right thing by his son…all those things touched her heart and made her love him.

Staring into his eyes, she tried not to let him see the revelation that had knocked her sideways. When had she first known the truth about her feelings? Only last night? Or had her regard for him grown almost imperceptibly in the weeks she had studied him in his element? Even during that first interview when he had been angry and borderline obstructive, she had been drawn to his masculinity, to his aura of command, and even to his arrogance.

Some men used their power and influence to ride roughshod over women and anyone they perceived as weak or inferior in any way. But Gil was different. He used his strength and capabilities to protect and support both his son and his wide circle of friends.

It hadn't escaped her notice that Gil was extremely popular in Royal. He was admired by women and respected by men. The truth was, in all her interviews, no one had ever spoken harshly or critically of Gil. He must have a few enemies or naysayers…most men in his position would. But if he did, she hadn't come across them yet.

Perhaps her mental "checkout" hadn't been as

long as it seemed. Because Gil waited patiently, his dark-eyed gaze a little too perceptive for her comfort. She didn't want him to know the truth. She didn't want him to think she was angling for something permanent. She didn't want him to think she would be kind to his son to win points.

"I enjoyed last night," she said quietly, her mouth dry and her throat constricted. "But I do have a job I need to attend to. It's late. I have to get back to town."

He frowned. "That's it?"

"What do you mean?"

"You can just walk away after last night?"

Her fists clenched. "What do you want me to say, Gil? It was wonderful. But we both have responsibilities."

"I'm tired of being responsible," he said, the words flat. "What I want is to go back upstairs with you and close the door."

Her heart raced. The image he conjured was unbearably tempting. "So would I," she said. "But that's not really an option, and you know it. Please let me go, Gil."

Something vibrated in his big frame and flashed in his eyes. Anger. Desire. He jumped to his feet and paced. "I'd rather you stay away from the club for a few days. Until some of the gossip and complaints die down."

She nodded. "I was almost done, anyway."

He folded his arms across his chest, looking more combative than amorous. "So why do you need to work today?"

"You are a stubborn man."

He shrugged. "I know what I want."

"If you must know, I had planned to speak with Alex again. The doctors only allowed me a brief moment with him when he was found, and of course, he remembered nothing."

"You think that has changed?"

"No. But perhaps on his home turf I can pick up some small clue…anything we might have missed earlier."

The ring of a cell phone interrupted them. Bailey glanced at Gil's phone where it lay on the table. "It's the sheriff."

"I'd better take this. Nate doesn't call to chit-chat."

Bailey listened unashamedly during the extremely brief conversation. When Gil hung up, she quizzed him. "Anything wrong?"

He nodded, sober-faced. "Alex was rushed to emergency during the middle of the night with an excruciating headache. And now there's some kind of uproar at the hospital. Nate asked me to get in touch with you and let you know."

Her mind raced. "Is Alex critical?"

"I'm not sure. Nate was in a rush and didn't take the time to explain. Do you think we should head over there?"

She nodded. "I certainly want to. Especially since Sheriff Battle was being mysterious. When do you have to pick up Cade?"

"Not until mid-afternoon. I'll drive you to the hospital."

"Thank you. But I'll take my own car. I don't know how long I'll be there. I don't want to be stranded when you leave."

He didn't like her choice. She could tell. But he didn't argue further. Instead, he pulled her to her feet, wrapped his arms around her and kissed her. Her arms circled his waist, feeling the heat of his body, the power, the ripple of muscle in his lower back.

His mouth was hungry, but gentle. They were essentially on display, though no one appeared to be close by at the moment. The broad light of day was far less protective of secrets, however, and far less private than a shadowy bedroom and a moonlit mattress.

She kissed him back, unable to resist. The way he held her conveyed so many things that hadn't been put into words. In his embrace, she felt not only desire, but also a tenderness that disarmed her.

His tongue teased the recesses of her mouth, making her knees wobble and her stomach tighten with pleasure. When she tasted him in return, he cursed quietly and set her away from him. The lines of his face were carved in frustration and thwarted need. "We're not done with this. Make no mistake."

Ten

Gil brooded on the way to the hospital, his hands wrapped around the steering wheel in a death grip. Only a short time ago he had awakened feeling jubilant and sexually sated and better than he had in a long, long time. A sleeping Bailey lay nude in his arms, her leg angled across his thighs, her hair a dark cinnamon cloud around her face.

He had held her close in the predawn darkness, deeply grateful for whatever path led her to him. She walked alone in life, it seemed. Halfway estranged from her father. No other close family. Though Gil admired her self-sufficiency, he wished she would not discount the possibility that her current assignment put her in danger.

The urge and desire to protect her was strong. As was the need to stake a claim somehow. That last bit didn't make sense. Bailey was not involved with anyone else sexually or otherwise. She might be staying at Chance's dude ranch, but Gil had no real worries on that score. Even if Chance made a move on her, Bailey would never get involved with someone who might be key in her investigation.

But still the urge remained.

Gil knew that some bridge had been crossed last night. Over the years, particularly when Cade was too small to realize that his dad was gone overnight, Gil had spent an evening with an amenable woman and had his sexual needs fulfilled. It hadn't taken very long for him to realize that such encounters left a sour taste in his mouth.

Apparently, he wasn't cut out for casual sex.

As a young man, before he had fully understood the extent of his wife's emotional trauma, he'd had every reason to believe that he and Sherrie would spend a life together at the Straight Arrow, potentially filling the house with a number of children.

Once the truth came out, Sherrie withdrew,

both physically and emotionally. Despite Gil's every effort, he had been unable to reach her. The loneliness of living in such a marriage hit hard, and had only increased tenfold after Sherrie's death.

Not even to himself had Gil admitted the great void in his life. It seemed ungrateful and almost wicked to complain when he had so many blessings. A happy, healthy son. A family property that generated a very comfortable lifestyle. A wide circle of friends.

But a man needed a woman in his bed at night. A woman by his side. A partner who would share dreams and sorrows and joy and troubles. Bailey seemed convinced that she was only passing through. And in truth, Gil had believed they had little basis for a long-term relationship. Their lives were so different.

But after last night...well...after last night, Gil was prepared to move heaven and earth to prove to her that she was wrong. He had no clear plan, no road map for avoiding the obstacles in their way. Nevertheless, he wasn't prepared to walk away from an experience and a woman who had made him rethink his monastic lifestyle.

A cynical person might point out that sexual euphoria was no basis for making serious life decisions. That simply because Gil had made love to Bailey Collins five times in one night didn't mean they were soul mates. That he was thinking with his male anatomy and not his brain.

Throughout history, sexual mistakes had brought down men with as much or more to lose than Gil. Sex often made fools of those who had the hubris to think they were invincible. Gil got it. He really did. But stubbornly, he believed his situation was different. That he and Bailey were different. They had connected last night with a fire and an intimacy that was as rare as it was stingingly real.

His thinking was muddled. There were things to be sorted out. And he felt as if he had a hangover, though he was stone-cold sober. But the future seemed brighter this morning. And for now, that was enough.

At the hospital, he parked and went to find Bailey. Royal Memorial was a modern, well-equipped facility outfitted with the latest in technology. Though Royal might not have the population of bigger towns and cities in Texas, there was plenty of money to go around, and the citizens had chipped in to endow various wings and such with generous gifts.

Bailey was waiting for him in the lobby. She had already checked with the information desk for the room number, so when Gil joined her, they headed for the bank of elevators.

"He's in a regular room," she said. "That's a good sign."

Gil kissed her cheek, hugging her briefly with one arm. They were alone in the elevator as they rode up. "I'm very proud of you, Bailey. Alex is a lucky man to have you on his side."

Her small smile was gratified. "Thank you. But until we bring this to a close, I won't be able to relax."

They got off on the third floor. A doctor was just coming out of Alex's room. Bailey flashed her badge and asked for an update.

The physician shook his head. "Not much to tell. We're running some tests, but the headache is most likely tied to the concussion. Not to mention the fact that Santiago is trying so hard to force himself to remember. I've cautioned him to back off. To rest. To give his brain time to heal. But patience isn't his strong suit."

Gil had known the doctor for many years. The man was, in fact, a longtime friend of Gil's parents. "Nate said there's some kind of commotion going on."

The doctor raised a bushy eyebrow, his expression slightly harried. "That's why we wanted to alert Ms. Collins. You might say there are some new developments in the case. And unfortunately, the sheriff was summoned away on an emergency."

Gil saw Bailey tense. "What kind of developments?" she asked.

"Mr. Santiago's father and sister have arrived from Mexico. The sheriff examined their credentials thoroughly before we allowed them to have access, though he has posted security guards, as you can see. Alex is awake and resting comfortably at the moment. We did give him something for pain, so he's a little groggy."

Gil put a hand at Bailey's back, following her into the room. By the window stood an imposing man with short, jet-black hair who bore a striking resemblance to the patient in the bed. The older man, probably in his mid-fifties, wore an expensive gold wristwatch and the kind of clothes that were made by a personal tailor. His brown eyes were not warm. Instead they had the flat, mud-like appearance of stagnant water.

Sitting in a chair by the bed was a striking young woman with long black hair. Her figure was curvaceous to say the least. A large, intricate necklace of thin gold filigree inset with deep burgundy rubies accentuated modestly revealed cleavage. The color of the stones was passionate. But their fire was not reflected in her face. She seemed exhausted.

"Who are you?" she asked, her voice deeply accented. "And why are you in my brother's room?"

Bailey stepped forward, hand extended. "I'm Bailey Collins, state investigator. I've been assigned to work the case involving Mr. Santiago's disappearance. And this is Gil Addison, president of the Texas Cattleman's Club."

The Latin beauty shook Bailey's hand briefly, her ample bosom confined in a jade silk dress. "Pardon my frankness, Ms. Collins, but from what Alex tells us about his ordeal, your progress in the case is, how do you say it…zippo. Nada."

Gil had to admire Bailey's self-control. She took the criticism without flinching. "I understand your frustration. But I can assure you that we are narrowing the field of suspects day by day. We *will* find out who did this." She paused. "I know the sheriff took a look at your identification, but I must ask to see it, as well. I'll need to scan it into our database as a precaution. I hope you understand that I can't merely take your word as to your connection with Alex."

The beautiful woman shot a look at the stranger by the window. "This is all his fault. Ask *him* about our IDs."

The older man ignored her.

Alex interrupted, his face etched in discomfort, his voice subdued. "Why would they lie?"

Gil watched in silence as Bailey eyed the visitors. After a brief hesitation, when Gil had the impression she was weighing her options, she offered her hand to the man, as well. "I'm pleased to meet you, Mr. Santiago."

The man's eyes flashed and he ignored her overture, forcing her to drop her arm. "Enough pretense," he hissed. "The IDs I showed the sheriff are fakes. My name is not Santiago. I am

Rodrigo del Toro." His voice resonated with arrogance and pride and a thick Spanish accent. "This is my daughter, Gabriella, and the man in the bed is my son, Alejandro."

Gil tensed. "Alex lied to us?" Alex had never talked about his background, particularly not the fact that he had family in Mexico.

Alex, looking almost frail despite his fierce masculinity, winced. "It's damned hard to answer that since I can't remember a damn thing."

Gabriella slapped his hand despite the fact that it was attached to an IV. "Language, *mi hermano*."

"Sorry." Alex grimaced. "I don't know who you people are, and I don't know why everyone thinks I'm Alex Santiago." His face reddened. "I'm trying. Hell, I'm trying!" The monitor beeped as Alex's blood pressure spiked.

A nurse came running, her brows drawn together in a frown. "I must ask all of you to leave the room. Mr. Santiago needs to rest. There is a small conference room at the end of the corridor. Feel free to continue your conversation there."

Alex's father and sister each kissed him on the cheek with muttered apologies, and walked out.

As Gil watched, Bailey approached the bed and laid a hand on Alex's shoulder. "It's not your job to figure this out," she said softly. "There are a host of people looking out for you, and many professionals working on your case. I need you to quit worrying about things and concentrate on getting well."

Alex's jaw tightened, his hands gripping the sheet at his hips. "I have no clue if that man and woman are related to me or not. I remember you asking me questions when I was found. Do you really not know who did this to me?"

"I don't. But I will. Let me do my job. And in the meantime, try not to push yourself to remember. Everything will sort itself out in the end."

Bailey approached the conference room with a sense of exhilaration. This new information had the potential to break her case wide open. Gil walked at her side, his quiet presence comforting.

Once seated at the small table, Bailey and Gil faced the del Toros. Neither of Alex's family members looked encouraging, though they did hand over their real driver's licenses and passports, albeit grudgingly. But Bailey had been stonewalled by the best, and she wasn't afraid of a little conflict. She pulled a small notebook and pen from her purse. Ordinarily, she would do an audio recording of an interview in addition to entering notes straight into her laptop. But she hadn't come prepared for that scenario, and even if she had, she doubted if the two people eyeing her with varying degrees of hostility would agree to going on the record at this point.

Before Bailey could pose a question, Gabriella leaned forward, her anger clear, though it was not perhaps directed at Bailey. "My father is to blame for this *horrible* situation. He sent Alex here as a spy. No wonder my brother was kidnapped."

Bailey turned to Rodrigo. "Is this true?"

The intimidating del Toro had ice in his gaze. She imagined that a man like him resented being cross-examined by a woman.

He leaned back in his chair, simulating calm, though his posture was rigid. "I assume that what I tell you is in confidence?"

She shook her head. "Not at all. If what you divulge to me is relevant to my investigation, I have to share salient points with other members of law enforcement. But you should realize…the more I know of the truth, the more quickly we can solve this case."

The scowl on his cold but handsome face darkened. "I sent my son to Royal to gather information about Windsor Energy. My company, Del Toro Oil, is interested in a corporate takeover."

For several long beats, silence reigned in the room. A quick glance at Gil told Bailey that he was as shocked as she was.

Gabriella's dark eyes shone with tears. Her voice quivered. "It was the most wicked idea. *Madre de Dios*, Father. Alex could have been killed."

Bailey fixed her attention on Gabriella's father, speaking sternly. She felt sympathy for the sobbing woman, but she also knew this was a chance she couldn't afford to miss. "Start from the beginning, Mr. del Toro. When was the last time you talked to your son?"

"From the accounts I have read in your newspapers, a couple of days before he disappeared. At the time, I did not know anything was wrong. We had agreed to be in contact only infrequently, because I wanted to keep a low profile."

"What did you talk about that day? Was it privileged information?"

His jaw tightened. "No. We argued. He told me that he had *una novia*, that he had proposed marriage to her."

"And you didn't approve?"

Del Toro pounded a fist on the metal table, once. But with enough force to make his daughter jump. "I am one of the richest men in Mexico, Ms. Collins. Alejandro is my only son. He is destined to marry someone of his class and background. Not the daughter of a man whose business I plan to grind into the dust."

"Charming," Bailey muttered. "So the woman of whom you speak is Cara Windsor?"

"Yes. She bewitched my son somehow. Alejandro has always honored and obeyed his father. Suddenly, he was shouting at me. Insisting that he could no longer carry out my plan, because he had to prove to this Cara person that his love for her was real. We have telenovelas in my country, Ms. Collins, somewhat akin to your soap operas. I have seen the overly romantic drivel that passes for true love. But the real world is not so easily manipulated. I expect loyalty and obedience from my son."

"How did your conversation end?" Bailey was chilled by the man's hauteur.

"He hung up on me. I did not know until almost a week later that he had disappeared."

"Why didn't you come forward immediately?"

"My son is resourceful. And I did not want to tip my hand. I assumed that he would show up eventually."

"And when he didn't?"

"I was packed and ready to hop on a plane when the news service indicated that Alex had been found."

"But without his memory."

"True. These things, however, are usually temporary. I had great hope that he would recall his purpose in coming to Texas and would carry on with the job at hand."

"And when it became clear that his amnesia was not going to clear up overnight?"

His jaw tightened. "I realized I had no choice but to come here and identify my son."

"When you walked into the room, did he show any signs of recognizing either one of you?"

Gabriella spoke up. She had been standing with her back to them, gazing out the window. She turned now, her cheeks streaked with moisture. "Alex knows nothing." Her voice was thick. "My beloved brother knows nothing."

The tears started again. Bailey's heart went out to the young woman. Though Bailey had no siblings of her own, she could only imagine what it must be like to have a loved one regard you as a stranger.

She tapped her pen on the pad, her brain whirling with questions. "Do you plan to stay here in Royal for any length of time?"

"I will not leave until my Alex is fully recovered." Gabriella's words were adamant. Her father appeared less sure.

"We will see what happens," he said.

"You may be very unpopular," Bailey pointed out. "Alex made many friends in his time here, but no one likes a mole."

"A mole?" he asked.

Though both del Toros spoke immaculate English, perhaps the slang did not translate. "An informant. A corporate spy."

Gabriella wrapped her arms around her waist,

her lashes spiky. "We need additional security for my brother, Ms. Collins. Now that the truth has come out, he will have more enemies. And whoever kidnapped him will no doubt realize that he is an extremely valuable asset, a bargaining chip if you will. They may try again."

"That will be a problem," Bailey said. "My employers are chronically understaffed."

Del Toro glared at his daughter. "Money is no object. I will hire bodyguards for Alejandro. And perhaps investigators of my own."

Bailey was startled to see Gil stand up, his face a thundercloud. "Watch your step, del Toro," he said, the words low and vibrating with anger. "This woman has spent more hours than you can imagine trying to find out why your son was kidnapped and by whom. You *will* give her the respect she is due."

The older man bristled, but he looked at Bailey and waved a hand. "I meant no insult. I am sorry if I gave offense."

As apologies went, it was weak, but Bailey accepted it at face value. She was stunned by Gil's impassioned defense of her work. Stunned and deeply touched. But she didn't need Gil fighting her battles. To allow him to do so would make her look weak.

She stood, gathering her things. "My job and my reputation are very important to me. And I have given my all to this case, though it isn't necessary for Mr. Addison to point that out." She scowled at Gil before continuing to address Alex's presumed family. "I appreciate your cooperation, Mr. del Toro. Ms. del Toro. I will have someone return your identification papers in the next hour or two. I assume you both will be staying with Alex?"

"If he will have us." Gabriella managed a weak smile.

Her father rose to his feet, as well. "My family will be together. And all of my resources are at your disposal, Ms. Collins. The sooner my son's attackers are behind bars, the sooner we can return home."

Eleven

Gil took Bailey's elbow as they walked across the parking lot. "Well, that was a surprise."

She nodded, her face troubled. "I felt like I was making definite progress with the investigation up until today, but del Toro's revelations put things in a whole new light."

"Does this mean Chance is off the hook?"

"I know you don't want to think he had anything to do with Alex's kidnapping. But I learned a long time ago that a surprising number of seemingly nice, normal people are capable of committing terrible sins in the heat of the moment. Chance certainly had motive."

"Because Cara broke his heart? You don't know that."

"True. And he doesn't act like he has a broken heart. But he could be hiding both his feelings and his guilt."

"We'll have to agree to disagree on the subject of Chance McDaniel," Gil said as he backed her up against the truck, his hips pinning hers to the door. No one was anywhere around. He bent his head and kissed her, sliding a hand around the back of her neck. "I wanted to stay in bed with you this morning," he confessed, his heart pumping as arousal brought his erection to full throttle.

Bailey's brown-eyed gaze clung to his. "I appreciated the privacy *and* your note. It was awkward enough as it was running into your housekeeper. I felt like I had a scarlet *A* on my chest."

He frowned. "Surely she didn't say anything to embarrass you." The woman had worked for him almost a decade, but he'd fire her on the spot if she had been rude to Bailey.

"Oh, no. She was lovely. But since you told me you'd never had a woman stay over, I felt extremely conspicuous."

"My housekeeper is not paid to speculate about my private life."

"People are human, Gil. She's probably discreet, because you're a good employer, but I *know* she was curious. Anyone would be."

"Change of subject," he insisted, kissing the side of her neck. "Tell me how soon we can be alone again."

Her wince gave him warning of what was to come. "With this new evidence," she said, "I have to buckle down on the case. I'll be spending time interviewing Alex's father and sister, assuming their story pans out. And I have to take a look at all my old notes in light of this new evidence. I can't have any distractions. You understand, don't you?"

She looked up at him so beseechingly, he had no choice but to swallow his disappointment and give her the support she deserved.

"I understand," he said, kissing the top of her head. "But I don't have to like it."

Bailey stroked her thumb across his bottom lip, her fingertips cool against his skin. "I'll make it up to you. I promise."

He backed away from her, reminding himself

that he was a grown man capable of delayed gratification. "I'll hold you to that," he said gruffly.

Fortunately for Gil, he was a busy man with many responsibilities. Even so, the subsequent week and a half dragged by with agonizing slowness. He and Bailey talked on the phone every day. Often more than once. But it was a poor substitute for having her in his bed…for feeling her naked body pressed against his. Somehow, without him even noticing, Bailey had become indispensable to his happiness. Without her, the days seemed dull, even with the presence of his precious son.

It didn't help that Cade asked about her constantly. The boy was single-minded in his determination to see her again. Gil made vague promises, but in truth, he had no idea when Bailey would be back under his roof.

On day eleven, he took matters into his own hands. Tracking her down took most of the morning. He finally found her vehicle parked at the courthouse…and waited with admirable patience for her to exit the building. When she saw him, her expression changed, but he couldn't pinpoint the mix of emotions that danced across her face.

Walking to meet her when she descended the steps, he slung an arm around her shoulders and steered her in the direction of his truck. He had parked in an adjacent alley, taking advantage of the shade from a large building, a spot that had the added benefit of giving them a modicum of privacy. "When was the last time you had a day off?"

"That's your best pickup line?" she quipped, smiling at him with joy in her eyes.

"Answer the question." He hadn't known for sure that she would be glad to see him. Witnessing her pleasure erased some of the misery of the past ten days.

Bailey toyed with the buttons on his shirt, her fingers warming his skin through the fabric. "I don't remember."

"That's what I thought. You need a break. I know for a fact that you've been working dawn to dusk."

"And what would I do with this free day?" She glanced at her watch. "Now that it's almost lunchtime?"

Gil was getting desperate. Making love to Bailey…repeatedly…had not slaked his hunger for her at all. If anything, he wanted her more, because now he knew what it was like to have her in his bed. The memories made him sweat. Not to mention the fact that he was, at the moment, hard and hurting.

Bailey made no effort to move. Obviously she was aware that his erection nudged eagerly at her lower abdomen. He shuddered, dangerously close to ripping open the door of the truck and shoving her on the front seat.

He cleared his throat. "Cade spent the night with my friends again. I have to pick him up. In Midland. At four." He was barely able to string words together. "Come with me."

Her head shake was instantaneous. "Your parental instincts were good…thinking you needed to protect your son. I don't want to do anything to hurt him."

"I was wrong. I'll be honest with him."

"And say what?"

"That I like you. A lot. And I like spending time with you. But that your job and your home are in Dallas."

"What are we doing here, Gil?"

In her eyes he saw a mixture of resignation and sadness. Both emotions hit him hard, because he was responsible for putting them there. He stroked her hair from her face, cupping her cheek in his right hand. "Let's not analyze it, Bailey. I'm a man. You're a woman. Let's take a drive on a beautiful sunny afternoon and worry about tomorrow later."

"That's a dangerously open-ended philosophy for a man like you. Or a woman like me, for that matter."

He made himself step backward. "I won't coerce you. But I hope you'll say yes."

She waited long enough for his gut to tighten. Finally, she nodded. "I suppose it couldn't hurt. But again, we both have a vehicle."

He groaned. "I'll pick you up at Chance's place in forty-five minutes. Change into something that will be comfortable for a picnic." The day was not as hot as it had been earlier in the week, but still wonderfully pleasant for January.

"Who supplies the food?"

"My invitation, my responsibility."

She went up on tiptoes and kissed him square

on the mouth, ducking away before he could grab her. "There's that nasty word again...*responsibility.*"

Gil swiped the back of his hand across his forehead. Bailey's kisses, even quick ones, were lethal. "Believe me, Bailey. Taking care of you and your needs is pure pleasure."

Bailey didn't have much time to dither over her wardrobe. But she did intend to prove to Gil that she wasn't all business all the time. He had used the word *comfortable*. Men, however, were clueless at times about what was appropriate. If Bailey and Gil were picking up Cade at the home of a family friend, there was a good chance Bailey would be meeting someone. And she didn't plan to do so in old jeans and a T-shirt.

The outfit she picked out was one that packed easily, but was comfy and fashionable at the same time. The short-sleeved, burgundy knit shirtdress was striped with navy and ended several inches above her knees. She paired it with navy leggings trimmed at the ankle with lace. Black espadrilles matched the black headband she used to push back her unruly hair. When she looked in the mirror after changing clothes hastily, the woman staring back at her definitely looked in the mood to play hooky.

Throwing a few things into a black tote, she gave her hair one last brushing and a warning to behave. Gil had seen her plenty of times with her hair confined for work. But because today he wanted her to let down her hair and goof off, she decided to indulge him both literally and meta-phorically. The only thing left was to grab up a black cashmere cardigan in case the weather turned colder later.

Gil was right on time. No surprise there. She walked down the wide front steps of the ranch house and tried not to bounce like a giddy teen-age girl. The prospect of a few hours away from work—in the company of the man with whom she had shared such dizzying intimacy—made her happy. A profound emotion, but one that was at its core plain and simple.

He helped her into the front seat of the truck and went around to the driver's side. "There's a belt in the center," he said, his lips quirking in a mocking smile.

Bailey smoothed her skirt over her thighs and

put her tote at her feet. "I'm fine right here," she said, staying well toward the passenger door. Midland was fifty miles away. Boundaries had to be observed if they planned to make it on time.

As they pulled out onto the highway, Gil shot her a look, his expression amused. "You look cute today, Collins. I like it."

She rummaged in her tote for a water bottle and took a long drink. "As much as I appreciate the compliment, I do want to point out that you promised to feed me."

"Patience, woman. The hamper's behind us, filled with all sorts of goodies."

She peered over her shoulder at the small space behind. Cade's little booster seat occupied one corner…a large rattan picnic basket, the other. "And how long do I have to wait?"

"There's a spot about twenty miles down the road where Cade and I like to stop. The property actually belongs to me, but I've never done anything with it. A tiny wet-weather stream cuts in in half. I thought you might like to have lunch beneath a little copse of cottonwood trees."

"You do know it's January. And all the leaves are gone."

"Use your imagination. I have a quilt."

"And sunscreen?"

"I'll cover you with my body."

Her jaw dropped and her face flamed. She'd been holding her own until that last comment. Now she lapsed into silence, her blood pumping with excitement. Surely Gil was joking.

Without asking, she reached forward and turned on his satellite radio. Picking an upbeat contemporary channel, she hummed along, relieved to have something to fill the silence. At times like this she realized that Gil was a man with one thing on his mind.

The turnoff to Gil's property was unmarked, nothing more than a narrow, rutted side road. The big truck handled the terrain comfortably, though Bailey was jostled rather more than she expected. If not for the seat belt, she would have ended up in Gil's lap.

When he finally stopped, at least four or five miles down the road, he rolled down the windows and cut the engine. "This is it."

The scene was peaceful, though remote. No one would disturb them. If another vehicle did approach, they would hear it coming long before it arrived. Above, puffy white clouds scudded across a sky the color of a robin's egg. A light breeze stirred the occasional flurry of dried leaves. With no power lines to mark the landscape, it almost seemed as if they had been transported back in time.

Bailey pressed her knees together, her hands clasped in her lap. "Very pretty."

Gil slung an arm across the steering wheel and turned to face her. "You look like a scared rabbit."

Bailey lifted her chin. "You flatter yourself."

His lopsided smile reached inside her chest and squeezed her heart. "I won't apologize for wanting you, Bailey. You're a very desirable woman."

Her cheeks were hot enough to fry an egg. She wasn't accustomed to talking about sex so matter-of-factly. She had been raised by a father who never did a thing to acknowledge that his daughter might need some education about her body and other personal matters. Nor did he offer her books or anything else to guide her in the murky waters of boy-girl relationships.

She'd been forced to stumble along on her own. But she had managed. Refusing to let Gil know she was feeling off-balance, she managed a genuine smile. "You promised me a picnic. Food first. Flirting later."

"You've got your priorities muddled," he grumbled. But he grinned as he unloaded their supplies.

Bailey hopped down from the truck and helped spread the quilt. Gil's housekeeper had managed to put together a mouthwatering array of food, especially given the short notice. Chicken salad, fruit salad, homemade bread and oatmeal raisin cookies made Bailey's mouth water.

She was astonished to see Gil unpack a padded container that held china plates, crystal flutes and real silverware. "Wow. I was expecting paper and plastic."

He poured her a glass of champagne. "I may be a little rusty when it comes to dating, but I think I remember a few of the finer points when trying to impress a woman."

She sipped the champagne, recognizing that the taste alone declared it to be ridiculously expensive. "We're not dating, Gil." She had information he wasn't going to like to hear. So there was no reason to play games. "But I appreciate the effort."

He ignored her insistence on clinging to reality, choosing instead to serve a plate and hand it to her. "Dig in. I don't want you passing out from hunger on my watch."

They ate in silence for several minutes. A comfortable silence that acknowledged the beauty of the day and their unspoken contentment in sharing a stolen moment in time. Bailey sat cross-legged, her plate in her lap, while Gil sprawled on his side, his big body ranged comfortably as he propped himself on an elbow and ate one-handed.

The food was good. But after a while, it sat like a stone in her stomach. She believed in the concept of carpe diem, she really did. But she was also a realist. For every wonderful minute she spent with Gil, there would be a corresponding experience of pain when this whatever-it-was came to an abrupt end.

It was foolish and self-destructive to ruin a lovely interlude with such maudlin thoughts. Life didn't have to be perfect to be enjoyable. Happiness came in snatches, sometimes almost unnoticed. She wouldn't ask of Gil more than he was able to give.

When they were done eating, she helped him pack everything back in its spot. They had barely spoken a dozen words during the meal. Gil stood and carried the hamper and the dish tote back to the truck. Bailey pulled her knees to her chest and encircled them with her arms. For one brief moment, she allowed herself to wonder what it would be like if Gil were hers. Permanently.

She already knew he was an incredible father and an intuitive lover. It wasn't a stretch to imagine him as a loving husband, as well. He had softened toward her, given more of himself than she had expected. Closing her eyes, she entertained the fantasy of a rosy future.

Gil sat down beside her, his hip inches from hers. "Whatever you're thinking about must not be too pleasant. You have a tiny frown between your eyebrows." He rubbed the spot with a fingertip. "This picnic was supposed to be fun."

Shaking off her weird mood, she laid her head on his shoulder. "It *is* fun," she said honestly. "I get so wrapped up in my work, I sometimes forget how nice it is to do nothing at all."

"You've given a lot of yourself to your career."

Was there a veiled criticism in those words, or was she being overly sensitive? "I suppose I've let my job act as a substitute for family. I do have many good friends, but we all work together, so that has a downside. I'm rarely able to leave my cases when I go home at the end of the day. Not like someone who works in a factory or a department store. I'm always thinking about the next step."

"You care deeply about things, Bailey. I like that about you."

She linked her fingers with his, resting their hands on his thigh. Today he wore dark dress pants with a lightweight cotton pullover sweater in a shade of blue that echoed the hue of the sky.

His words of praise made her uncomfortable. Perhaps because she had grown up without that kind of verbal support. But also because she was hiding something from Gil. News she had received only today.

"Did you bring me out here so we could have sex?" she asked, the words far more calm that the riotous emotions pinballing inside her.

He squeezed her hand, his thumb massaging her palm. "It might have crossed my mind."

This would be their last chance. She knew it, and she was pretty sure Gil knew it, too. Their lives were too complicated to carry on an affair, clandestine or otherwise. Especially in a place like Royal where even the walls had ears. Turning to face him, she cupped his neck in her hands and pulled him closer for a kiss. "I was hoping you would say that."

Her blunt statement sent shock skittering across his face before it was replaced by hunger and determination. He reached into his pocket and extracted a series of condom packets hooked together. "I wasn't making any assumptions, but it never hurts to be prepared."

"Don't tell me. You were an Eagle Scout."

"Guilty as charged." He unbuttoned the top two buttons of her dress. "I also learned how to unhook a girl's bra with one hand, but that wasn't a Scout badge. More of an extracurricular activity."

"You're not such a straight arrow after all, are you Mr. Addison? I'm seeing you in a whole new light."

He eased her down onto her back with her co-operation. The sun blinded her, so she was forced to close her eyes.

His lips caressed her ear as he whispered. "You have no idea."

Twelve

Gil studied Bailey's face...the creamy skin, feminine nose, stubborn chin. In the broad light of day, her hair caught every ray of sun and glowed red with fire. Her slightly parted lips were the color of pale pink roses. Beneath her soft dress, her chest rose and fell rapidly.

In his head, the clock was ticking. He'd called his friends and asked for an hour of grace. Cade was having a blast and wouldn't begrudge the later arrival time.

Selfishness. All selfishness. Because Gil couldn't bear to let her go. Not without one last chance to bury himself in the tight, hot clasp of her body. To hear her cry out when he sent her flying. To lie with her in the aftermath and count the beats of his heart.

She had kicked off her shoes when she sat pretzel-fashion to eat her lunch. Now he studied her narrow, highly arched feet, bemused that the sight of them made him wonder for the first time if he had such a fetish. Her small toenails were painted the same color as her lips.

A tiny smile curved her lips. "I have my eyes closed, so I can't be sure. But it seems as if you've lost your way."

He stood and pulled her to her feet. "Your skin is turning pink. Let me move the quilt." With trembling hands, he dragged it into the patch of shade cast by the truck. "That's better."

When he turned back around, Bailey had pulled her dress over her head and stood facing him clad only in a lacy black bra and the leggings that clung to her shapely limbs.

He put a fist to his chest. "Be still my heart."

"Not that I'm criticizing, but it seems like one of us needs to remember the clock."

"I don't have to be there 'til five. I called them."

Her eyebrows went up, her expression scandalized. "You asked your friends if you could be late so that you and I could fool around in the middle of nowhere?"

He shrugged, not the least bit repentant. "That's about it."

She threw herself across the small space separating them, forcing him to catch her by the waist and lift her against his chest. He staggered backward, but caught himself.

Laughing down at him, her eyes sparkling with an innocent joy he'd rarely seen compared to her serious side, she rested her hands on his shoulders. "I do like this naughty version of Gil Addison. Very much."

For that, she deserved a kiss. Slowly, he let her slide down his body...like the hero's maneuver in a romantic chick flick. Her breasts nestled against his chest, giving him a mouthwatering view that was more provocative than total nudity. When her feet touched the quilt, they were both breathless. He tunneled the fingers of one hand in her hair, grabbing a handful and pulling her close. "And I do like this bra."

She rested her cheek on his shoulder. "I'm waiting to see your fancy maneuver." Grabbing his left hand, she brought it to her lips. "Show me what you've got."

To his eternal embarrassment, it took him three tries to unfasten the bra clasp one-handed.

Bailey just laughed. "I think I'm glad you aren't any better than that. No woman likes to be part of a crowd."

He pulled her down to the quilt again, this time knowing that nothing was going to stand in his way. "You'll never be one of a crowd, honey." She didn't know how true that was, but now was not the time to convince her with words.

He knelt over her, dragging the belt from around his waist and tossing it aside. Thankful that he hadn't worn his boots today, he kicked off his shoes and socks and unfastened his trousers. His erection bobbed thick and ready, tenting the thin fabric of his boxers.

Bailey licked her lips. "This feels wicked," she murmured.

"What does?"

She waved a hand. "Doing it outside in broad daylight."

"All the better to see you with, my dear."

"So that makes you the Big Bad Wolf?"

He grinned, shucking the pants but leaving the boxers for now. His sweater was far too warm, so he dispensed with it, as well. Bailey's interested gaze studied him from head to toe and all points in between. Her unconcealed perusal aroused him even more, if that were possible.

"You could say that," he said calmly. "I do have an inclination to gobble you up. Lift your fanny, woman." He peeled her leggings down and off, exposing thighs and calves that were long and shapely. The black lace panties he revealed matched the bra that now lay nearby.

He shook his head, trying to dispel a rush of dizziness, possibly caused by all the blood that had traveled south.

Bailey bent one knee, placing her foot flat on the quilt. The new position was provocative to say the least. "You okay?"

He nodded, hands on his thighs. "I need a minute. Looking at you may give me a heart attack."

"Very funny."

"I'm not kidding," he insisted. "Have you seen yourself in a mirror? You're a knockout, Bailey."

"It's the champagne talking. I may have to drive to Midland. I think you're delusional."

Trapping her thighs between his, he straddled her waist. The rocky ground beneath the quilt was hell on his knees, but the pain was a good thing if it kept him from rushing the moment. "Don't argue with me. I'm always right."

"You like to think so."

"If I kiss you, will it shut you up?"

"Why don't you try it and see?"

He crouched over her, stroking her curves with hands that trembled. Though the afternoon was plenty warm, small nipples pebbled at his touch. Despite her saucy bravado, he detected a hint of shyness even now. Her eyelids fluttered shut as he played with her breasts.

Her hips moved restlessly. He recognized the signs and felt the same urgency. "I want to make love to you," he said, the words ragged and hoarse. He felt as if he could barely draw a breath.

As she lifted up on her elbows without warning, she brushed the underside of his erection. "Then we're both going to get what we want." Her smile was pure female mischief.

Wiggling her hips, she used one hand to remove her last tiny scrap of underwear. He stood and followed suit. Donning a condom, he dropped down beside her and splayed a hand on her belly. "You dazzle me," he said roughly, with perfect truth. When he had fallen in love with his wife-to-be, he had been no more than a callow young man, hardly aware of the pitfalls that could loom in a relationship.

His marriage, or rather its failure, had almost broken him. When Sherrie ended her life, Gil had drowned in pain and guilt. During Cade's brief lifetime, things had gradually improved, because Gil had willed it to be so. But he had been convinced deep down inside that he would never have another chance at love.

Yet without warning, Bailey Collins had burst into his life. First he had resented her. Then he had wanted her. And now...he could barely even describe to himself what it was that he was feeling.

Bailey smiled at him wistfully, her eyes dark, mysterious. Was she even a fraction as hungry as he was?

Her hand wrapped around his erection, moving gently up and down, her fingers circling the head of his shaft. "I will always be glad I came to Royal," she whispered. Her voice broke on the last word.

"Don't say that. Don't write an epitaph before we're done."

Her eyes glittered with moisture. "Time's running out, Gil. Come here and give us both what we need."

He obeyed blindly, because joining his body with hers was what he wanted more than his next breath. Touching her gently, he felt the slick heat that signaled her readiness. He thrust slowly, closing his eyes at the sensation of rightness. Somehow he had to make this new turn in his life work. Somehow…

The sun moved inexorably in the sky. Already the rays burned his back, the patch of shade shrinking. Each of his senses was painfully heightened. Bailey's skin was soft and warm everywhere he touched. The sound of their breathing mingled and floated away on the breeze. He smelled the fragrance of her perfume and the scent of his own sweat.

He withdrew briefly, though it cost him. Lightly, he teased the tiny spot that gave her the most pleasure. Her back arched off the quilt and she cried out as she climaxed, her body beautiful in its sensual abandon.

Before the last ripple of her orgasm faded, he entered her again, this time with far less finesse. Wildly he took her, over and over, until he felt a scalding rush of heat that ripped through his gut and drew a harsh shout from his parched throat at the end as he came endlessly, his head buried in the curve of her neck.

Bailey peeked through half-closed lashes, eyeing the buzzard that circled far overhead. Had she and Gil been comatose that long? She lifted her hand and squinted at her watch. Almost four o'clock. By the time they put themselves to rights and finished the drive to Midland, Cade would be waiting on them.

She nudged her lover's shoulder. "Gil."

"Hmm?" He didn't stir.

"We have to go."

"I bought us an extra hour," he mumbled.

"We've used that and more. I'm serious. Move, Addison."

He levered himself up on one elbow and blinked.

"Crankiness is not a nice trait in a woman," he said. "Maybe you could work on that."

His droll humor made her smile. "Duly noted."

He helped her to her feet and she leaned into him, relishing the intimate feel of skin-to-skin contact.

Gil pinched her bottom. "I'd kill for a shower."

"Yes, well…you're the one who opted for alfresco shenanigans."

"You're the only person I know who could use that word with a straight face." He kissed her nose.

"It's a perfectly good word."

"Do they teach you that in law enforcement training?" He lowered his voice. *"I've got a sixty-two fifty-one down at the Motel Six. Shenanigans without a license."*

She burst out laughing. "You are so full of it. Get dressed before someone comes to arrest us."

They were woefully unprepared for the aftermath of their romp. Fortunately, Gil remembered a container of wet wipes in the glove box. With the aid of those and the items in her purse, Bailey was able to restore her appearance to some semblance of dignity and decorum. Though she had left home looking perky and fresh, she was now definitely disheveled.

It didn't help that Gil kept trying to snitch her bra or tweak unprotected body parts. And that was not the only distraction standing in her way. Who could help noticing the breadth of his muscled shoulders or the fact that even now, he was semierect. As if his hunger had been only partially sated by their coupling.

But at last, they finally climbed back into the truck and headed out to the highway. When they made it onto even pavement, Gil shot her a look. "I have a favor to ask."

She pulled down the visor mirror and checked her reflection, wetting her finger to remove a tiny bit of something stuck to her eyebrow. "I'm pretty sure you used up all your markers back in Dry Gulch."

"I'm serious."

"Okay." She closed the mirror. "Tell me."

"I'm meeting up with a friend tomorrow morning and helicoptering three counties over to check on some stud bulls we hope to buy. I use a high school girl in town to babysit Cade in the evenings whenever I need her. But it occurred to me that he would really enjoy spending part of the day with you. Chance has activities for children out at the ranch, doesn't he?"

"Yes. But you don't have to do this. I don't need a grand gesture to prove that you trust me with your son. It isn't necessary."

"So you don't want to hang out with him?"

She sighed. "Of course I do."

"Then what's the problem?"

Now seemed as good a time as any to share the news she had been sitting on since midday. "I talked to my boss when I went home to change clothes."

"You called him?" Gil's jaw was tight.

"No. He called me. Apparently as soon as we left the hospital, Rodrigo del Toro did some digging and went up the chain of command. He informed my boss that he would assume responsibility for the investigation since he had unlimited funds and Alex was safely back at home."

The word Gil said under his breath was harsh. "So that's it? The state drops the case without a resolution?"

"No, of course not. But del Toro doesn't like working with a woman, and he holds the purse strings right now, unfortunately. They'll send someone else to step in for me here in Royal. And besides, I'm needed back in Dallas to take over a new case."

"When?" It wasn't her imagination. He was pale beneath his tan.

She swallowed, feeling on the defensive and not sure why. "This coming Thursday. I have to wrap up all my notes and file a final report."

"I see."

The next few miles passed in uneasy silence. She didn't understand Gil's reaction. It was no secret that her assignment in Royal was temporary. Perhaps Gil was angry because Alex's kidnapper hadn't been apprehended.

"I don't think you have to worry about public safety," she said, after at least fifteen minutes had elapsed on the dashboard clock. "We're almost ninety percent sure that Alex was targeted specifically. This isn't some rogue criminal who poses a threat to the general population. And now that Mr. del Toro is here—with money to spare for security details—I think any real danger is minimal."

"For Alex's sake, I hope you're right." Even

after her earnest reassurances, his shoulders were still rigid, his hands white-knuckled on the steering wheel.

She bit her lip. Confrontation had never been her strong suit. But in ten minutes or so, the talkative Cade would be joining them. Before that happened, Bailey wanted to clear the air.

"You seem upset," she said.

Gil's scowl was dark. When he took his eyes off the road for a brief moment to look at her directly, the turbulence in his gaze shocked her. "And you're not?"

"I don't understand."

With a jerk of the steering wheel and a flurry of gravel, he pulled off onto the side of the road and shoved the gearshift into Park. Turning to face her, he shocked her with the vehemence of his icy tone. "Maybe I can explain it in words that make sense to a by-the-book government type."

"That's not fair," she said, tears stinging her eyes.

"Too bad, because that's how I see it." He was furious, that much was clear. "Your boss summons you, and it doesn't bother you at all that you and I are in the middle of a—"

She punched him in the chest, halting the flow of heated sarcasm. "I *know* what we're in the middle of," she cried. "But we both know the statistics on long-distance relationships."

His lips twisted, his expression bleak. "So we were merely scratching an itch?"

"Don't be crude." She was shaking. Wrapping her arms around her waist, she held on to a thread of composure. "When we were together before… and again today. It was wonderful."

"The sex, you mean." His eyes were flat, accusing.

"What do you want from me, Gil?"

The silence lengthened. "Nothing, Bailey. Nothing at all."

Thirteen

She didn't know what to do. Never in a million years had she expected this reaction to her announcement. Inside, she grieved for the moment she would have to say goodbye. Of *course* she was sad. The thought of leaving Gil was tearing her apart. But moaning about it wouldn't help.

He moved back out onto the highway, merging with the traffic and eating up the miles to Midland.

The hostile silence shredded her nerves. "Tell me about your friends," she said. Anything to pass the time until Cade would join them. With the little boy in the truck as a buffer, the trip home wouldn't be so bad. At the moment, however, her head was throbbing, and she needed a distraction sooner rather than later.

For several long seconds she thought Gil was going to ignore her request. But finally, he inhaled and exhaled, and some of the tension left him. "We all went to college together," he said. "Got married about the same time. Had a son about the same time. They were an incredible support to me after Sherrie was gone. Food. Companionship. Advice when I asked. A shoulder to cry on."

"I can't imagine you letting down your guard enough to admit you needed help." It was a true statement, but as soon as the words left her mouth she realized they came out sounding sarcastic. Fortunately, Gil didn't take offense.

"I was a mess," he said with raw honesty. "I was still adjusting to being a parent, and I was terrified I would do something wrong. Plus, the guilt about Sherrie was overwhelming."

"It wasn't your fault."

"Doesn't matter how true that is or how many times you tell yourself so, the burden is crushing when someone you love commits suicide. I felt like a complete failure."

Only hours ago she would have slid across the seat and put her arm around him. Now, she didn't feel as if she had the right. "I'm glad they were there for you."

"My parents were, too. They still lived in Royal back then."

Bailey stared out the window. She was under no illusions that her father would ever rush to her aid in a similar situation. The divide between them was much too large to cross.

Perhaps that was why she hadn't let Gil see the depth of her despair about leaving Royal…about leaving him. She had learned early on in life to pull herself up by her bootstraps and deal with hardships on her own. Self-sufficiency had been one of the few things of value her father gave her. That and the certainty that if she ever had a child of her own, she would wrap him or her in love that would never be doubted.

In the midst of her soul-searching, the truck rolled to a stop in front of an attractive two-story home in an upper-middle-class neighborhood. Bailey touched Gil's arm. "I'm going to stay here." He had already told her he didn't plan to linger.

Gil frowned. "Don't be ridiculous. Come meet my friends."

She shook her head. "They're an important part of your life. If I go in with you, they'll make assumptions. Let's not complicate things."

"Lord, you're stubborn."

"Go get Cade. I'll be fine."

He stalked away, clearly displeased. Her decision was the right one, though. If Gil showed up with a woman in tow, his friends would think something was going on. And it wasn't. She and Gil were having recreational sex. To fill a void in their lives.

Wanting more didn't make it so.

As Gil walked back to the truck with Cade, he ruffled his son's hair. "I have a surprise for you."

"What is it?" Cade looked tired and not quite as bouncy as usual. No doubt the boys had stayed up far too late.

"I brought a friend with me."

Gil opened the truck door and helped Cade climb into the back. The boy grinned hugely when he saw who sat in the passenger seat. "Hi, Miss Bailey. Wish I could sit up front with you."

She leaned over the seat and patted his knee. "We have to obey the law. Wouldn't want Sheriff Battle to arrest us."

Gil climbed in behind the wheel. "What is this obsession you have with being arrested?" he asked, the words barely audible.

Wincing, she remembered using the very same words only an hour before…when she and Gil had stood stark naked beneath the afternoon sun. She closed her eyes, still able to see in her mind's eye the two of them tangled together on an old, dusty quilt.

Ignoring Gil's provocative mutter was her only option. "I have an idea," she said. "Why don't I ride in the back with Cade? That way he won't be all alone."

Cade squealed with delight even as his father's face darkened with frustration. "If that's what you want."

Cade chattered nonstop three-fourths of the way back to Royal, and then without warning fell sound asleep, his little body slumping against Bailey's shoulder trustingly.

Her eyes met Gil's in the rearview mirror. "Poor thing is exhausted."

"Well, I haven't slept much for the past ten days. And you don't seem to be worried about me."

"Gil!"

"I'm not going to let you pretend nothing happened, Bailey. Things are different now."

"How?"

Fortunately for her, the question stumped him. Either that or he wasn't willing to talk about it in front of his son. Her blunt question put an end to any conversation at all. She leaned her head against the window and dozed, enjoying the feel of Gil's son pressed up against her side.

It was getting dark when they made it out to McDaniel's Acres. Lights in the farmhouse created a welcoming glow. Cade never stirred when Gil opened the passenger door and helped Bailey climb out of the backseat.

When her feet hit the ground, he continued to hold her. "We have to talk about this. But now is not the time."

Her heart swelled with hope and longing. Was he going to tell her something important? Something that could change her life forever? For the better?

She knew he was right about timing. Serious conversation required privacy. But when he bent his head and kissed her so very gently, she wanted to blurt out the truth. *I love you, Gil.*

Any anger and frustration he felt had melted away or had been stuffed into a box marked Don't Spoil the Moment.

She strained against him, feeling the urgent hunger that was never far from the surface. He didn't try to hide his arousal. Knowing he needed and wanted her was almost enough. But not entirely.

Wrapping her arms around his neck, she tried to read a deeper meaning into his tenderness. Did he feel anything for her beyond simple lust?

At last he released her. Breathing harshly, he rubbed a thumb over her cheekbone. "Don't fret, sweetheart. Everything is going to be okay. I promise."

What did that mean? What was he planning?

Before she could press for answers, he was gone…the taillights of his truck shining red in the gathering darkness as he headed home with his young son.

She walked up the steps slowly. Would it matter if she asked her boss for one more week? Or would that simply prolong the pain of walking away from Gil?

It startled her to realize that Chance was sitting on the front porch swing. And he was not alone. Cara Windsor stood abruptly. To Bailey's trained eye and with the illumination from the porch light, it was easy to see that the beautiful blonde had been crying.

Before Bailey could do more than say a quick hello, the other woman dashed down the steps, got into her car and drove away.

Chance spread his arms across the back of the swing, his long legs outstretched. "Was that Gil I saw bringing you home?"

Her cheeks flamed. She and Gil had kissed on the far side of the truck. Chance couldn't have seen much. But it was still embarrassing. "Yes. I rode with him to Midland to pick up Cade."

"Cute kid."

"Yes."

"I hope you haven't planted doubts in Gil's head about me."

What could she say to that? "Gil makes his own decisions. And he's very loyal to his friends."

"Yes, he is. But men can do irrational things when a woman is involved."

Here was her opportunity. She dropped her tote on the floor and leaned against a post. "Is that what you did, Chance? To be with Cara?"

The smile faded from his face. "Things aren't always what they seem, Bailey. To be honest, I had no idea I was still on your list."

"She's not wearing her engagement ring anymore, is she? I like you, Chance. But it's hard to overlook the fact that she's been hanging around here instead of helping her fiancé regain his memory. Is there anything you want to tell me?"

He stood in one fluid motion and faced her, topping her by several inches. His move could have been threatening. But in her gut she knew it wasn't. "You've already questioned me, Bailey. Twice, if I remember correctly. And I told you everything I know about Alex's disappearance. Which is pretty much zero."

"And was everything you told me about Cara the truth? Did you perhaps leave out some pertinent details?"

"I did not. There's nothing more to tell."

"That tête-à-tête I interrupted a few minutes

ago didn't look like nothing. Why don't you tell me what you were talking about? Why was she crying? Was it because the man she thought she loved doesn't even know who she is? Is that it?"

He folded his arms across his chest, his expression grim. "Cara's business is her own. If you want answers, you'll have to ask her."

"She didn't look like she wanted to talk to me."

"Perhaps not."

"I'm not the bad guy in this equation. Unless of course you really are guilty. In which case, you're out of luck. Because I never give up until I solve a case." She winced inwardly, because technically, that wasn't true. Not this time. Thanks to her boss, she was not going to have the satisfaction of finishing *this* investigation.

"At the risk of looking guilty when I change the subject, I'd like to give you some advice."

"Okay. I'll bite. What is it?"

"Gil Addison is a hell of a nice guy. And he's had some rough knocks. He deserves to be happy more than most anyone I know."

"And this concerns me how?"

"Don't let your passion for the truth hurt him. If you're not serious about a relationship, then walk away."

* * *

She pondered Chance's pointed remarks as she climbed the staircase to the second floor where her room was located. Was she giving up too easily? Did Gil believe he and Bailey had a deeper connection than she was giving them credit for?

Tossing her tote and sweater on the bed, she pulled her phone from her pocket and saw that she had a text from the man who filled her thoughts so completely.

Is it possible for u to meet me at the club in the morning...11:00 a.m....so I can hand over my rambunctious son??

She frowned as she curled up on the window seat. Under the circumstances, she would rather not see Gil again until she'd had time to process her emotions. But she had made a promise, and she couldn't disappoint the child caught in the middle of an adult conflict.

No problem. 11 it is. What will he want for lunch?

Gil's reply was swift.

Anything that ends with ice cream.

She tapped the keys.

So the diner would be good?

Definitely.

Resisting the urge to ask him what he meant earlier when he said everything would be okay, she added one last note.

See you then...

She set the cell phone on the bedside table and began changing out of her dress and leggings. Moments later, the text alert dinged again. Curious, she glanced at the screen.

My bed looks empty without you...

Torn between caution and excitement, she debated answering. Perhaps he would think she was in the shower if she didn't respond.

A second *ding* heralded another message.

I know you're reading this. I can feel your anxiety all the way over here. Quit worrying.

Easy for him to say. Since she couldn't think of an appropriate answer, she stood there staring at the prompt…

What we have is more than good sex, and you know it.

Her lips curled in a reluctant smile. How long would he carry on a one-sided conversation?

It's going to be a long, uncomfortable night. Every time I close my eyes and think of you, sleep is the last thing on my mind…

Finally, bravely, she replied with what was in her heart.

I miss you, Gil…

This time the long silence was on his end.
After two full minutes, his answer came.

I miss you, too, sweetheart. Sleep well...

Gil plugged his phone into the charger and prowled his bedroom, pacing from one side to the other. He'd told Bailey the truth. Everywhere he looked he saw her. Naked, sprawled across his mattress. Laughing. Panting. Crying out when he made her come.

How could two incredible sexual encounters turn his entire world upside down? Before he had gotten to know this woman, he had learned to live with loneliness, with sexual deprivation. Hard work and dedication to his son's welfare had enabled him to forget—most of the time—that he was a man in his prime, a man who had the same needs as any other man.

Now that the genie was out of the bottle, though, there was no way he could go back to the way things were. He stopped dead in the middle of the room, struck with the knowledge that he was falling in love with Bailey Collins already. His subconscious must have known long before now, because the intensity of what he was feeling didn't happen overnight.

He'd been so busy stonewalling her and arguing with her that it had taken him all this time to admit she was exactly the woman he wanted. She was tough and strong and not afraid to do what was right. She was gentle with his son and passionate in Gil's arms.

The fact that she wore boring suits with naughty undies enchanted him. Knowing that she was a positive, upbeat person in spite of her sterile upbringing only added to his admiration of her character.

He couldn't wait to see her again. Was the emotion he had seen in her eyes this afternoon more than simple hunger?

Was it possible that Bailey cared about him in return?

He considered himself a fairly intuitive person, though he'd be the first to admit that women were complex creatures. Was Bailey leaving because Gil had given her no reason to stay?

From her perspective, he'd done nothing concrete to say that he wanted her in his life permanently. It shamed him that she could believe he saw her as no more than a good time.

The fact that she had a job and a life in another city complicated things. Was there any point in trying the long-distance thing for a while? Gil couldn't walk away from the ranch that was his son's heritage and his family's roots. Not to mention the fact that the Straight Arrow provided a considerable number of jobs.

But was it fair to ask Bailey to give up everything and Gil nothing? He had a lot of thinking to do and not much time to do it. With Bailey being summoned home on Thursday, he had less than a week to analyze his gut feelings and make a plan. And then there was Cade. Gil was pretty sure what Cade's reaction would be, but he needed to sit down with his son and tell him what was going on. That his father wanted to include Bailey in their family.

Imagining the three of them as a unit healed a lingering hurt in Gil's soul. A dream had been stolen from him tragically long ago. Now he had a chance to start over, to have the traditional family he had always envisioned.

As he showered and climbed into bed, he realized that he was far too wired to sleep. By this time tomorrow night, God willing, he and Bailey would have an understanding. Perhaps he could fly to Dallas with her when she went back and they could shop for a ring.

He would use any means in his power to make her happy. Everything was going to be perfect.

Fourteen

Bailey arrived in town fifteen minutes early. She was genuinely looking forward to spending the day with Cade, but even more than that, she wanted to see Gil. His mysterious promises had lit a tiny flame of hope deep inside her, hope that he felt the same connection, the same craving to make their relationship more than a passing fancy.

When Gil's familiar big truck pulled up at the club, he and Cade hopped out. The two males were dressed similarly, both wearing jeans and cowboy boots with light rain jackets. The skies were dull, and the forecast called for showers.

Gil's coat was black to match his hair. Cade's was bright blue and reflected his eyes.

The boy ran across the pavement. "Hi, Miss Bailey! I get to stay with you today."

She grinned, kneeling to hug him. "Yes, you do. And I'm excited about that. I thought we'd start with lunch if that's okay with you."

"Yes, ma'am." Cade beamed.

Gil touched the child's shoulder. "Take my phone and sit on the bench over there for a minute, please. You can play that new game we bought. I need to talk to Bailey."

Cade did as he was told, leaving Bailey and Gil to face each other. She felt self-conscious about being seen by club members, given their location. When Gil smiled at her, though, all that faded away.

He reached out to touch her, but apparently thought better of it at the last minute, because he retracted his hand. "I want to kiss you, but I don't want to embarrass you," he said.

"It *is* a fairly public spot. Maybe later?"

"No maybe about it." His gaze roved her face, his eyes burning with hunger. "I didn't sleep worth a damn."

"Me either."

They stared at each other.

He raked a hand through his hair. "I want us to talk. Tonight. Serious stuff."

"Sounds scary, but okay."

"When you bring Cade home this afternoon, stay for dinner." He paused, a spark of devilment in his brown eyes. "And breakfast. You can stay in the guest room if it will make you feel better. But you should know that Cade sleeps like the dead."

"Won't it look odd if I bring a suitcase with me?"

"Throw a few things in a shopping bag. He won't pay any attention, I promise."

Joy bubbled in her chest. There was no mistaking his meaning. This was as good as a declaration. "In that case, I'd love to come."

He glanced at his watch. "I've got to get going. You'll be okay with him? If he gets too rowdy, time-out usually works."

"Don't worry. We'll be fine."

Bailey held Cade's hand as his father backed out of a parking space and drove away with a wave. She glanced down at her charge. "You ready to eat?"

Cade nodded enthusiastically. "I'm starving."

The kid could put away a lot of food. After consuming a full-size hamburger and a mountain of ketchup-laden fries, he declared himself ready for dessert.

"What does your father allow you to have?"

"Two scoops of ice cream with chocolate sauce and one cherry."

"A man who knows his own mind."

Cade cocked his head. "What does that mean?"

She grinned. "It means you are definitely your father's son."

After a brief rain shower that left the air sticky and the ground damp, the skies began to clear. Out at McDaniel's Acres, Cade was in his element. He had grown up on a ranch, so much of the activity was familiar to him. But because Chance's place was geared toward tourists, there were extras to entertain a young boy. Pony rides, a miniature rodeo-themed playground, and best of all, a new litter of puppies out in the barn, just begging for someone to play with them.

Fortunately the little canines were old enough to be away from their mother some of the time. Cade sat entranced, holding two of the six in his lap. They were mixed breed, part hound and part terrier.

For a young child, Cade was remarkably patient. He stroked their ears and talked to them with such sweetness that Bailey was hard-pressed not to get teary-eyed. She'd never been allowed to have pets as a child. A moment like this was one she would have treasured.

Cade looked up at her. "Which one is your favorite?" he asked, very serious.

Bailey studied the pups carefully. "That one," she said. "The smallest one with the black patch on his ear."

"He looks like a pirate."

"I agree. If he belonged to me, I think I'd call him Captain Jack."

"Do you have any pets, Miss Bailey?"

She shook her head. "I have to travel a lot for my job, and it wouldn't be fair to leave an animal at home alone."

Cade looked up at her with his trademark grin. "Whenever you're at my house, I'll share my pets with you. I have two dogs and a hamster."

"That's a very nice offer."

"Dad told me before he left today that he asked you to come to dinner at our house tonight."

She gnawed her lip. "Yes." She wasn't sure she was ready for this conversation.

"Do you like him?"

It was ridiculous that she felt her cheeks warm. "Of course I do. Lots of people like your dad. He's a nice man."

Cade rolled his eyes, looking like one of the precocious kids from the Disney Channel. "Miss Bailey, you know what I mean. Do you want him to be your boyfriend?"

She squatted beside him, hands on her knees. "I thought we talked about this."

"I'm not asking for a new mom. I just want to know if you like him."

The kid should be a lawyer when he grew up. She studied his innocent face, his features so like his father's. "Some subjects are for grown-ups, Cade. It's not that I don't want to answer your question. But what you're asking me is a private thing. Between your dad and me. Do you understand?"

His sigh was theatrical. "I guess so." He rubbed the puppy's head, his eyes downcast. "He likes you."

Oh, crap. How dignified was it to pump a kid for information? But the temptation was too much. "How do you know?"

Cade's expression was earnest when he looked up at her. "I heard him singing in the shower this morning."

Bailey frowned. "So?"

"So my dad never sings in the shower."

"Maybe he was in a good mood."

"I told you. He doesn't sing in the shower."

Clearly, Cade's logic made perfect sense to him. But Bailey was befuddled. "I'll take your word for it," she said. Reminding herself that she was a mature adult, she derailed the provocative conversation. "Let's go back to the house. Chance's cook promised to fix a snack for you."

Cade stood up, a piece of hay stuck to his pink, round cheek. He tucked his small hand in hers as they walked back to the main house. "I like you, too, Miss Bailey. Thanks for babysitting me today."

* * *

An hour later, Bailey took Cade up to her room and washed his face and hands and removed the worst of the mud from his shoes. She couldn't return him to his father looking like a ragamuffin. "We'd better head out," she said. "If I'm late getting you home, I'll be on your dad's bad list."

Cade giggled. "Dad says people aren't bad. But sometimes they do bad things. Is that how you get on the list?"

She picked up his jacket and the small cowboy hat Chance had given him. "I suppose so. Your dad is a very wise man." And a darned good father. Cade's maturity and grounded personality didn't happen by accident. It was the result of unwavering love and the confidence he possessed that his father would always protect him.

Her car was warm from sitting in the sun. She cranked up the air and then made sure Cade was properly strapped into his booster seat in the back. His eyelids were drooping. He considered himself too old for a nap, but he had played hard today.

As the crow flew, the trip from Chance's ranch to Gil's wasn't all that far. But the only way to get from one to the other was to drive the several miles out to the highway, hang a right for another six or seven miles, and finally, traverse the long road out to Gil's house.

The whole trip took thirty minutes or so. Cade, bless his heart, was conked out before she even got to the main highway. Keeping the radio turned low, she hummed along to a favorite song, feeling her pulse race at the thought of being with Gil again.

Imagining what he wanted to talk about was tantalizing. But she kept her anticipation in check. It was a long time until Cade would be tucked in tonight. By the time she and Gil talked, it would be late. After that, would he expect intimacy? With his son asleep down the hall? Or would they go their separate ways?

She couldn't imagine that. Not after yesterday. Gil looked at her with such intensity in his gaze that she was under no illusions about what he was thinking. He was a virile man. A sexy, masculine alpha male. And he wanted *her*.

The knowledge was exciting. But she felt restless and nervous. The sting of continuous desire was a unique experience. She didn't know it was possible to feel such gut-level need and still be so uncertain about the future. Would tonight be a watershed moment? Or was she making too many assumptions?

Suddenly, seemingly out of nowhere, a car pulled out to pass her. She grimaced. Impatient drivers were the worst. In slow motion it seemed, she glanced in the rearview mirror to look at Cade and almost simultaneously realized that the vehicle beside her was not merely crowding her accidentally. The driver jerked his wheel sharply and sideswiped her, pushing her toward the side of the road.

Her training clicked into gear. She had to outrun them. But even as she stepped on the gas, she despaired. The car responded sluggishly, the front right tire hung up in the ditch. With shaking hands she grabbed her cell phone and texted 9-1-1 to Gil…and seconds later to Nate. Then, *dialing* 9-1-1, she dropped the phone on the front seat and left the call open.

Her heart in her stomach, she prayed that Cade would stay asleep. The thought of him being scared made her angry. When she determined that her car would go no farther, she put it in Park. Bitterly regretting that she had not brought her service weapon, she debated her options. If at all possible, she would not let whoever had disabled the vehicle get near Cade.

At the moment, there was no movement from the other car. It had stopped, as well.

She glanced at Cade. His thumb was in his mouth and he clutched the small plastic pony that was his favorite. But still he slept.

Adrenaline flooded her stomach with sickening force as the door of the other car swung open and a man exited the vehicle. He wore a ski mask. Walking rapidly, he closed the distance between them. Though his arm was not outstretched, he had a gun in his hand pointed at the ground. "Get out of the car," he said loudly, standing several feet away, nothing but glass between them.

"What do you want? I have money." She reached for her purse. "Credit cards. Cash. Take it and leave me alone."

"Let me see both of your hands."

Her brain raced. Did he know she was trained law enforcement? Was this Alex's kidnapper? Slowly, wanting to draw his attention away from Cade, she held up her arms.

The man's posture was rigid. "Get out."

If she did as he asked, Cade would be completely helpless.

The man took two steps closer. "Now," he shouted. "Or I shoot the kid." He placed the muzzle of the weapon against the glass of the back window.

Bailey glanced desperately at the boy in her charge. "Cade," she whispered. Knowing she couldn't take a chance that the man was bluffing, she unlocked the door and stood up. The assailant charged her and struck the side of her head, and her world went black.

Gil flew down the street toward the sheriff's office. He'd been in the chopper, still a long way out from the airport when Bailey's text came through. His return call to her went straight to voice mail.

Parking his truck haphazardly, half on, half off

the sidewalk, he jumped out and ran toward the building just as Nate pulled up in a squad car, sirens blazing. Gil stared at his friend, his heart pumping like a madman's. Before Nate could speak, Gil grabbed his arm. "What in the hell is going on? I got a 9-1-1 text from Bailey."

"Me, too."

"Damn." Fear like he had never known swept over Gil. It was a hell of a time to figure out that his love for Bailey was neither halfhearted nor theoretical.

The door to the building burst open and Nate's second in command ran to meet them. "A 9-1-1 call came in about forty-five minutes ago. From Ms. Collins. She left the connection engaged so we could listen in. As crazy as it sounds, it appears that someone tried to carjack her. We sent personnel out immediately."

Nate frowned. "Where?"

"We located her cell phone signal. She was about halfway between McDaniel's Acres and Mr. Addison's place."

Fury choked Gil. "Where in the hell were you, Nate?"

"On a domestic disturbance call north of town. Woman took a butcher knife to her husband. I got back as soon as I could."

The cell phone at the young man's hip crackled. He answered it, and the blood drained from his face. "I understand. Thank you."

Gil felt a great yawning void in his chest. "Tell me," he said hoarsely. "Tell me."

The twenty-something kid swallowed visibly. "They found the car. Ms. Collins was lying in the road…unconscious. Nasty blow to the head."

"And my son?"

The younger man was pale as milk. "He's gone, Mr. Addison. No sign of him."

Gil reeled mentally, though he kept himself upright by sheer strength of will. Everything seemed very far away, the street sounds muffled.

Nate took his shoulders and got in his face. "Steady, man. We're going to find him."

"He's only a baby." Gil had spent the past five years making sure his son was happy and healthy. "How could this happen?"

The deputy spoke up, his voice shaky. "We have a team going over the crime scene. They're very good."

Nate still held Gil's shoulders. "Why don't you go to the hospital and check on Bailey? I'll text or call you every half hour. We have a protocol, and we're going to be all over this. Trust me, Gil. I'll search for that boy as if he were my own son."

Gil wanted to argue. He wanted to get in his car and comb the county. But without a lead, he was stonewalled. "You have to find him. I can't lose my son. I can't lose my son."

Nate released him, but still frowned. "I'm not sure you should be driving."

Gil glanced at his car. "I'm fine," he said dully. "I'm fine. I want to go with you." Everything inside him screamed in agony. The woman he loved was hurt…badly. But Cade needed him. The cruel impossibility of helping them both sliced him to shreds.

Nate hesitated, obviously weighing the pros and cons of letting Gil ride shotgun. "It's boring work," he said. "We'll be there for a while."

"Doesn't matter. I might be able to help."

"Fine. Let's go."

Gil saw nothing of the familiar scenery as it flashed by his window. When Nate screeched to a halt in front of three other squad cars and a van, Gil saw Bailey's car. Bile rose in his throat, but he choked it back.

They got out, and he strode beside his friend, stopping only when he saw the unmistakable stain of blood on the ground. *God in heaven.*

Nate quizzed the detective in charge. "Tell me what you know."

A female officer, her eyes shadowed as she glanced at Gil, spoke calmly and concisely.

"The damage to the victim's car indicates that someone sideswiped her, forcing her off the road. We have decent tire tracks, as well as several shoeprints. Assailant was likely male.

"Any blood *inside* her car?"

"No."

Gil walked on shaky legs toward the vehicle and peered inside. "His booster seat is gone."

Nate followed him. "That's a good sign. Whoever took the boy means no harm."

Just then another officer climbed out of the mobile lab in the van and jogged up to them, his face red from exertion. "We found this, sir."

He handed it to Nate. "It's a tracking device. No telling how long it's been on her car. We're trying to find the manufacturer."

Fifteen

Nate cursed as Gil's blood congealed. Gil squeezed the bridge of his nose, his fear mounting. "I told her that what she was doing put her in danger. She wouldn't listen."

Nate shook his head. "This may have nothing to do with Alex's disappearance."

But Gil could hear the uncertainty in the sheriff's voice. The timing was too much of a coincidence. Someone could have kidnapped Cade, knowing that the wealthy Alex Santiago would pay to ransom a child's life. And now that Gil knew the truth about Alex… Good Lord. If the attacker knew the truth, also, then he or she was aware that del Toro was one of the richest men in Mexico.

Gil cleared his throat. "A kidnapping for ransom would be a best-case scenario. If that's what happened, they won't hurt him." But Gil's innocent son would still be scared and alone. *Goddamn it*.

Nate pulled out his phone and dialed. "I'm calling the hospital. If Bailey wakes up...*when* Bailey wakes up," he said more forcefully, "she may be able to give us a description of the car and the attacker. In the meantime, we'll put out an Amber Alert."

"But with no vehicle description and no way to tell who Cade is with, that will be pretty useless." Gil's fury was misplaced. Nate was trying to help. They all were.

Gil spun on his heel and strode down the road, away from the vehicles, away from the image of his son being dragged from the car, away from the sickening vision of Bailey lying in the dusty road.

When he had put several hundred yards between himself and the uniforms, he stopped, eyes scrunched closed against the piercing pain that threatened to explode his skull. *Dear God,* he prayed. *Protect them...please...* His brain was in such turmoil, those were the only words he could articulate. Over and over. *Protect them. Protect them.*

Nate followed him moments later. "I need to know what he was wearing."

Gil rattled off the requested information, trying not to think about how he had helped Cade get dressed only that morning, the little boy chattering excitedly about his day with Bailey.

Nate answered a call and listened intently. When he hung up, he touched Gil's arm in a brief gesture of reassurance. "Bailey's going to be okay. She has a severe concussion and required several stitches. It was a bad wound, but she's stable. The head nurse will call me when they have further news."

"I don't know what to do." The six words ripped his throat like sharp glass. His whole adult life he had been a man in control, the one to whom everyone else turned in a crisis. What kind of father stood by helplessly while his child faced God knew what evil?

"I think you should go to the hospital now. Call

me with updates about Bailey, and I'll keep you apprised of our progress here. It's going to be critical that we find out what she knows."

Gil understood the sense of what Nate was saying. But he had the odd and terrible notion that he needed to stay right here. At the spot where his son was last alive and well. As if by some miracle, Cade might teleport back to Bailey's car and this whole thing would be a dream.

He nodded slowly, his hands fisted at his sides. The sense of helplessness was suffocating. But if he could not help his son in the short term, his only other option was to be with Bailey.

He had closed his mind to the possibility that she could have been killed. He couldn't process that thought in the midst of his son's disappearance. The brain could only handle so much trauma before it shut down. Bailey was fine. And she would understand his delay.

Leaving the crew on the scene to search for any last clues, Gil and Nate headed back into town. Gil got out of the squad car and stood on the sidewalk. It was a beautiful evening. All around them traffic bustled. People smiled and waved. The world went on.

But for Gil, time had stopped.

Nate hugged him. An unusual enough occurrence that Gil was both shocked and taken off guard by the other man's compassion.

Nate stepped back, preparing to go inside. "I'll keep you posted, and you do the same."

Gil nodded.

"Talk to someone at the hospital. You may be in shock. You won't do anyone any good if you collapse."

"I'm fine. Really." It was true. He was encased in ice now. Nothing could touch him. He had a plan and a mission. Watch over Bailey. Find out what she knew.

Leaving a concerned Nate staring after him, Gil strode to his truck, climbed in and started the ignition. For a moment, he couldn't remember which way he needed to go to find the hospital. Realizing that Nate still watched him, Gil took a deep breath and shifted into drive. He backed up, pulled into traffic, and rounded the corner.

Five minutes later, he pulled off into a narrow alley, put his head on the steering wheel and sobbed.

* * *

Had it been only a couple of weeks since Gil and Bailey had visited Alex? Kissing her in the parking lot seemed like a dream now…a bitter-sweet dream. Tonight was supposed to have been a threshold for them, a day of reckoning. Instead, anticipation had crumbled into sickening fear for his son.

Gil walked into the hospital, sparing only a fleeting thought to wonder if Alex had been dis-charged. Thinking about Santiago…or del Toro… or whatever his name was made Gil's anger rise again. It wasn't Alex's fault that Cade was gone. Gil knew that intellectually. But it was easier to shift his fury onto Alex than to admit that he had failed his son.

The waiting room was empty. Gil approached the pleasant-faced older woman volunteering at the information desk. "Bailey Collins. Can you tell me her room number?"

"Are you family?"

He ground his teeth. "She has no family in the area. I'm her friend."

"I'll need to check with the nurse…"

He gripped the edge of the desk, closing his eyes briefly and reaching for patience. "Ms. Collins and I are in a relationship. Do you understand what I mean? I have to know what's going on."

The lady in the pink smock flushed, her eyes wide. "I'm just following rules, sir. But I will take you at your word."

While Gil waited, the woman made a brief phone call, then hung up. She smiled hesitantly. "Ms. Collins is not in the room. She's having a CT scan and a couple of other tests as a precaution. As soon as she's back, they'll let me know."

Gil swallowed, feeling light-headed. "Thank you." Numb and filled with a black void of despair, he dropped into an uncomfortable chair on the far side of the room. A TV on the opposite wall, thankfully muted but with closed captioning on, played old reruns of *The Andy Griffith Show*. Opie was small in this episode, maybe Cade's age. He had broken his arm falling out of a tree, and Sheriff Andy was carrying him into the hospital.

Seeing the tears on Opie's face broke through

Gil's calm, letting in a torrent of rage and terror. He dropped forward, head in his hands, elbows on his knees, and prayed.

An hour later, a doctor approached him. Gil leaped to his feet, swaying when spots danced in front of his eyes. He had skipped lunch knowing that the housekeeper was preparing a big spread for tonight's dinner with Bailey, hosted by Cade and himself.

It was after eight now.

The man stared at him with the same compassion Gil had seen in Nate's eyes. "Mr. Addison?"

"Yes."

"Your friend is back in the room resting."

"May I see her?"

"Only for a moment. She's had something to help her relax and sleep. We're monitoring the concussion."

"Are you aware of the situation?" Gil asked, his throat tight with a combination of frustration and dread.

The doctor nodded. "You need her to wake up. I get it. But you have to understand that her body needs rest and peace to heal. If she regains consciousness right now, she'll have to relive every-thing that happened, and she'll become agitated. At this critical juncture, I can't allow that. I'm sorry, Mr. Addison. Hopefully if her vital signs are good tomorrow, I can reconsider."

When the man departed, Gil pulled himself together and followed the directions back to the Bailey's room. Standing in the doorway, he felt his vision blur. Struggling to stand up straight, he moved toward the bed.

She lay still as death, her skin unnaturally pale. A large bandage covered an area that included her temple. An IV was secured in the hand that rested atop the sheet. Gil stared at that hand, re-membering how it had caressed him.

Knowing Bailey, she would have done every-thing to save Cade. But it hadn't been enough. Bailey hadn't saved him, and neither had his fa-ther.

Emotion roiled in him, hot and deep. This was the woman to whom he wanted to propose mar-riage. By all rights he should be sitting at her elbow, promising to remain by her side.

But though every cell in his body wanted to hold her and comfort her, a sick guilt held him back. How could he think about loving Bailey when the only other person he loved with equal intensity was out there somewhere? Alone. Terrified.

A male nurse stepped in to check BP and temp and adjust the flow of medication. "She's doing as well as can be expected, sir. It was a nasty wound."

Gil leaned against the wall. No one told him she had cut her face. A neat line of stitches closed a gash on her forehead. She must have hit a rock or some other sharp object when she fell.

"Should I leave my number?" he asked, his lips numb as he formed the words. He felt as if he were outside his body observing.

The man nodded, moving about the bed with efficient, gentle motions. "Write it on the board, if you will. Someone will get in contact with you if there is any change. If you'll permit me to give you some advice, sir, I'd suggest you go home and get some rest. You look pretty bad. Visiting hours start at ten in the morning. There's nothing you can do for her now."

Gil didn't remember walking back to his truck, but he found himself behind the wheel. In some dim corner of his brain, he realized that he was impaired. Driving as slowly as a geriatric en route to Sunday church, he made his way home, determined not to hurt anyone else.

Though it was cold, he sat on the back porch to call Nate. But there was no news. The investigation was ongoing. They were doing everything they could to find Cade.

The housekeeper had gone home. She left instructions for heating dinner. Gil fixed a plate of chicken casserole and ate five or six bites. Moments later he was in the bathroom throwing up.

He couldn't walk upstairs. He couldn't look into his son's bedroom. He couldn't look at the bed where he and Bailey had made love with such happy abandon.

His soul in ashes, he stretched out on the sofa in the living room and slung an arm over his eyes.

Bailey didn't want to wake up. Somewhere just offstage, pain waited, deep and vicious. She clung to the drug-induced fog, well aware that the alternative was not something she wished to face.

Hours passed. Maybe weeks. She didn't know.

She didn't care. Nothing could hurt her in this wonderful cocoon.

But eventually, her cowardice was challenged. Professional voices, sympathetic but demanding, insisted she accept reality. Swimming toward the surface, she noted the various aches and pains that held her down. The crushing throb in her skull was the worst.

She opened her eyes cautiously. The light was bright. Too bright. Turning her head slowly, she focused her eyes on the man sitting by her bed. Frowning, she tried to decipher what was wrong with the picture. "Nate?" she croaked.

The sheriff jumped to his feet, looking down at her with an indecipherable expression. "Let me get the nurse," he said.

"No, wait." She frowned. "Why are you here?"

He rubbed a hand over his chin. "I wanted to see how you're doing."

"Gil?" The omission of his name seemed ominous.

"He's on his way." The answer was too quick, too hearty.

She closed her eyes, sifting through the layers of memory. A hospital. Something had happened. Suddenly, the truth crashed down on her. A wail ripped from her throat. "Cade," she cried, her head pounding. "What happened to Cade?"

Nate went white, and suddenly the room was filled with medical personnel. Seconds later, the fog returned…

Gil and Nate stood at the foot of the bed. Bailey's doctor was there, as well. The older man's expression was grim. "We've backed off the sedative. You'll have to be quick. This morning her BP skyrocketed when she realized what had happened."

"What if she can't help us?" It was Gil's worst fear. He had hung all his hopes on the fact that Bailey would be able to explain things when she woke up.

Nate shifted from foot to foot, his gaze watchful. "We'll work with what we have."

Slowly, almost imperceptibly, Bailey returned to consciousness. The first sign that she was at all aware of her surroundings was the frown that creased the space between her eyebrows.

The doctor looked at the monitor. "She's in

pain. As soon as you have what you need, I'll give her more meds."

Gil shuddered. What they were about to do seemed little shy of torture. "You have to do it," he muttered to Nate. "I can't. I'll step over here where she won't see me."

Nate stared at him. "I understand."

As Gil watched, Bailey opened her eyes. Only for a few seconds. But in a moment, she tried again, this time focusing on Nate.

He spoke softly, reassuringly. "Hey, there, Bailey. Glad to see you're back with us."

Her lips trembled. "I'm so sorry."

Nate touched her hand. "Steady. I need to know if you can help me. Do you remember?"

Her expression destroyed Gil. He had never seen such agony on a woman's face.

"Yes," she whispered.

Nate nodded, his face calm, his eyes kind. "Someone ran you off the road and hit you on the head."

"Yes."

"Who was it?"

"I don't know. He wore a ski mask."

"Anyone else in the car?"

"I think so, but I'm not sure."

"And the vehicle?"

"A beige sedan…newer model. Maybe a Honda. The plate was dirty, but it was Mexican, I think. Had a 367 at the beginning."

"Anything else, honey?"

"It all happened so fast. They didn't want money. Cade was in the car asleep. I had to do something…" Tears welled in her eyes and spilled down her cheeks. "Oh, God." She sobbed aloud, groaning as her involuntary movements caused her discomfort.

Nate squeezed her hand. "Relax, Bailey. It's okay. You may remember something else later. Everything's going to be okay. I promise."

The doctor pushed something in the IV and Bailey's body visibly relaxed.

Nate exhaled. "Well, at least we have something. It's a start."

Gil shook his head, his heart sick. "It's damn little."

"Faith, Gil. Keep the faith."

Sixteen

The next time Bailey awoke, she knew exactly where she was and why. Gil sat beside her bed, his eyes closed, his face gray with exhaustion. She wet her dry, chapped lips. "May I have a drink, please?"

He roused instantly, poured water from an insulated pitcher, and stuck a straw in it. Holding it for her, he helped her take several sips. "You look a little better," he said.

"You don't have to stay with me. I know you have responsibilities at the ranch. And you need to help Nate look for..." Her throat hurt. She couldn't say the last word.

He shrugged. "They tell me civilians only get in the way."

She closed her eyes, processing what he wasn't saying. "You're angry with me."

"No." The answer was quick. "But I warned you that the investigation was dangerous."

His calm stoicism made her feel worse. Inside, he had to be a mess. And all because he had entrusted Bailey with his son's care, and she had allowed him to be kidnapped.

"Is there any word about Cade?" She could barely voice the question. Because she knew the answer in her heart. Gil wouldn't be here if Cade had been found. He would be with his son.

Gil's expression was grim. "Not yet. Nate has brought in off-duty officers from other counties. I'm footing the bill for the extra help. They will find Cade."

"You sound so sure."

His gaze met hers square on, and for the first time, she saw the extent of his torment. "I can't allow room for doubt. I won't." His voice was raw.

Tears burned her eyes, but she blinked them away. "I never should have let myself get close to you or to Cade. We're all paying for my self-ishness."

His scowl deepened. "We both made mistakes. Both lost sight of our primary goals. You had a job to do, and I had a son to protect. Have a son," he corrected swiftly, the words cracking.

A masculine voice in the hall caught her attention. It sounded like the sheriff. Gil stood up. "I'm going to grab a cup of coffee. I'll be right back." He pulled the door partway closed as he walked out.

The men conversed in low voices, obviously thinking Bailey could not hear them. But she was able to catch words here and there, enough to piece together what was being said.

They were arguing about possible theories. Judging from Nate's line of thought, he was still expecting a ransom note. She strained to listen. Gil was audibly upset, his voice growing louder.

Suddenly, the voices moved away and the hall was silent.

Bailey shrank back in the bed, tears filling her eyes and spilling across her cheeks. Gil would never forgive her, even if and when Cade was found. Her actions had brought harm to Gil's family. One moment she'd been standing on the cusp of something wonderful, and now it was all gone.

The pain made it hard to breathe. She loved Gil Addison and his son. But she had lost them both. Shaking and cold, she punched the button to summon the nurse.

Moments later, the woman entered the room, her expression concerned. "Are you hurting? It's not time for medicine yet."

Bailey *was* hurting. Her dreams had shattered into a million pieces. Now was a heck of a time to learn that a heart truly could break.

She gripped a handful of the sheet, her breathing choppy. "Is it okay if I limit my visitors?"

The woman frowned. "Of course. Is there a problem?"

"I'm willing to see the sheriff. But no one else. Please."

The woman's eyes were kind. "Would you like me to ask the chaplain to come by?"

"No." Bailey's throat was so tight she could barely speak. "Thank you." She couldn't bear to look into Gil's eyes and see his anger and disappointment and fear. It was better to make a clean break.

"I'll make sure your wishes are noted at the nurse's station and on your door."

"Thank you."

The woman left. Bailey turned her head to stare out the window. The sun was shining brightly, in direct opposition to her bleak mood. How soon would she be able to travel? Her boss needed her back in Dallas, and Bailey wanted to go home. If there was more work to be done in Royal, she would ask to be reassigned. She couldn't come back here.

In her heart, though, she knew she would not be able to leave until she had the assurance that Cade was back in his father's arms…safe and happy. Thinking about the alternative was unbearable. Surely a ransom note would arrive soon. One victim with no memory, one child too young to plan an escape, and Bailey—who had been unconscious when the child was taken. It was an impossible situation.

Her brief burst of energy faded, leaving her drowsy and deeply sad. Cade had trusted her. Gil had trusted her. And she had failed them both. The knowledge haunted her.

She drifted into sleep, her dreams dark and threatening. Suddenly, she was back on the road between Chance's place and Gil's ranch…

She felt the cold slither of fear. The rapid beat of her heart. She stared at the man. He was tall. Maybe older. But the ski cap obscured every-thing important. Think, Bailey. Think. She fo-cused on the car. It was ordinary. A figure sat in the passenger seat. Again, she saw Cade, sweet innocent Cade in the backseat. Then, something brutally hard hit her head. She crumpled, the ground coming up to meet her.

Bailey woke with a start even as the recol-lection of panic pushed adrenaline through her veins. The bland sterility of the hospital room was recognizable and reassuring. With shaking hands, she pushed the button to call the nurse.

Gil sat beside Nate in the squad car as they sped through town. "I don't understand. Why didn't she call *me?*" he asked

"Don't know." Nate slowed down for a stop sign, noted the empty side streets, and kept going.

He had his lights flashing, but the sirens were off. At the hospital, they parked in a restricted zone. Both of them jogged toward the front of the hospital.

On Bailey's floor, a nurse with salt-and-pepper hair stopped them. "Hello, Sheriff. Mr. Addison."

Gil shifted from one foot to the other, impatient to hear what Bailey had to say. And to see for himself if she was improving. "We're here to see Bailey," he said, wanting to add, *Get out of my way, woman.*

"I'm sorry, sir. Ms. Collins has restricted her visitors."

Gil looked at her blankly. "What the hell does that mean?"

The nurse frowned at his language.

Nate touched his arm. "Take it easy." He addressed the woman calmly. "I had a message that Ms. Collins wanted to see me."

"She does. But Mr. Addison, I'm sorry. You can sit in the waiting room down the hall."

Gil felt his temper rise. He was on a short fuse from worry and lack of sleep. "I think there's been some kind of mistake," he said, injecting ice into his voice.

The woman didn't budge. "She was very clear. Only the sheriff."

Gil's eyebrows shot upward, incredulity in his exclamation. "I was here a few hours ago. What's this about?"

Nate gave him a glance. "Keep your mind on the goal, buddy. Let me go in and see what she has to say."

Relief washed over Bailey when she saw Nate's head poke around her door.

"You ready to see me?" he asked.

She nodded. "Pull up a chair."

When Nate made himself comfortable, Bailey managed a smile, though she hoped it didn't look as false at it felt to her. "I think I remembered something. It may amount to nothing. So don't get your hopes up. But then again, it might be a lead."

He leaned forward, elbows on his knees. "Tell me."

"I'm almost positive there *was* another person in the car that ran me off the road…a woman in the passenger seat. I remember seeing long hair. And today, something clicked. What if this has nothing to do with Alex? What if Gil's in-laws took the boy?"

Nate's gaze sharpened. "That's an angle we haven't considered."

"Were you in Royal when Gil's wife died?"

"Yes."

"So you remember that his wife's parents tried to get custody of Cade? And nearly succeeded?"

"True. But Gil hasn't heard from them in almost five years. I still think someone might have been sending you a signal to get out of Royal."

"You're probably right. But it won't hurt to check this out, will it?"

"I won't waste any time." He got to his feet, leaned down, and kissed her gently on the forehead. "Thank you. Now concentrate on getting better. That's an order."

"Yes, sir."

He stopped at the door and turned, his expression no longer as excited. "Why won't you see Gil?

"My reasons are private."

"You might want to cut him some slack. He's been through hell. Worried about you. Sick about Cade."

"I understand what's at stake here. But I'm not

Gil's responsibility. He needs to focus on his son." She was proud of the even tenor of her voice and the calm expression on her face.

Nate shrugged. "I've seen the way he looks at you, Bailey. What's a man to do when the two people he cares most about are in harm's way at the same time?"

"I'm not upset with him, Nate, truly. Cade needs to come first. That's as it should be."

The sheriff looked as if he wanted to argue with her, but the clock was on her side. "You have a new lead to follow," she said. "Quit wasting time here."

"Can I let Gil come in to see you?"

She shook her head, her chest tight. "No, thank you. I'm going to take a nap. Please let me know when you have any news."

The door shut behind him, and finally she could release the tears that had been building.

If Gil had learned nothing else in this crisis, it was that he didn't like twiddling his thumbs. A man needed action to feel that he was making progress. *Hurry up and wait* was a special kind of torture.

One of the deputies brought him a cup of coffee. "There's a cot in the back room, Mr. Addison. It may be a while before we hear anything. Maybe you could sleep for an hour or so."

Gil managed a smile. "Thank you. I'm fine." He'd lost track of the number of hours he had been awake. Sleep had been nothing more than moments of lost consciousness every now and then. His eyes were gritty. His body ached. And a great yawning emptiness filled the space where his heart had been.

He had truly thought Bailey would be part of his life. But now he wasn't sure. Had she picked up on his ambivalence? His guilt over wanting her when Cade was missing? God, he felt as if he were being stretched on a rack. In dark moments when the fear for his son threatened to make him go mad, he escaped into his memories, seeing pictures of Bailey in his bed.

The images sustained him and gave him hope. But now he had lost Bailey, too. If he had to, he would give his life for either one of them, his son or his lover. But what if he didn't get that chance? What if his life was reduced to nothing but emptiness? Would he ever recover?

Nate answered a phone call, his demeanor intense. He looked almost as tired as Gil. But a weary smile lit his face when he hung up. "They have the full license number. And the vehicle it's associated with belongs to your wife's parents. We've sent the information out statewide, and across the border, as well. It shouldn't be long now."

"Unless they've ditched the car and are hiding out."

"They must have been keeping tabs on you for a long time. When they realized you were getting close to Bailey, they started tracking her, as well. I'm betting they planned every possible scenario. A deserted road would have seemed like their golden opportunity."

Gil leaned against the wall, his body suddenly limp with fatigue. "Tell me we'll find him, Nate."

"We will," the other man replied, the two words allowing no room for doubt. "We will."

The next time Bailey awoke, the sky outside her window was dark, and Nate had returned.

She scanned his face. "Any news?"

He shook his head. "No. But we're cautiously

optimistic. Your theory about the grandparents was right on target. What we *don't* know is
whether they took Cade immediately across the
border or if they've hidden out somewhere here
in the states to avoid detection. The Mexican authorities are assisting every way they can."

"I see." It was a tiny comfort to know that she
had been able to provide some help, after all. But
it wasn't enough. The larger question loomed.
Was Cade safe? Dear God, let it be so.

Nate yawned, and she glanced at the clock on
the wall. "Please go home if you can," she said.
"I'm feeling much better, and the night staff
nurses are wonderful. I'd appreciate it if you
would keep me updated."

He stood and stretched. "Of course."

"Thank you for all you've done."

He gave her a lopsided smile. "Gil is my friend.
And you're a very nice woman. It's what we do
here in Royal."

After he left, she pondered his words. It was
true. She had seen it time and again since she had
been assigned here. The community was tight-
knit. And they would go out of their way for one

of their own. What must it be like to have that kind of security? That depth of loyalty?

Her friends back in Dallas were all great people. But they were spread out across the city. Bailey didn't live with the kind of neighborly closeness that thrived here in Royal.

She was lucky that for the moment they were including her in the circle. It was a warm feeling. And one she wouldn't mind replicating.

The nurse came in to check her vital signs and also to give her a pain pill. Bailey had insisted on reducing the dosage. She didn't like being so drugged, and the throbbing in her head had subsided somewhat, at least enough that she could sleep. She punched her pillow into a more comfortable shape and tucked her hand under her cheek. When she turned out the light, she felt entirely alone.

Seventeen

Gil loitered at the end of the hallway until he was sure his presence would go unnoticed. Bailey's room was dark. He slipped inside and quietly pulled a chair close to the bed. Gently, he touched her head.

Stroking her hair lightly so as not to wake her, he whispered the words he had wanted to say long before now. "I love you, Bailey."

Though he had barely made a sound, she moved restlessly in the bed and opened her eyes. "Gil? How did you get in here?"

A tiny light on the panel above the bed was the only illumination in the room, but it was enough for him to see the wariness in her expression.

He shrugged, unrepentant. "I sneaked in when no one was looking." He took her hand. "How are you feeling?"

"Much better. I think they're going to release me in the morning."

"Why did you shut me out, sweetheart?

She withdrew visibly. "I want you to go." Her voice quivered.

"Please, honey. Tell me the truth."

Her big eyes were tragic. "I can't bear to see the look on your face. I know you blame me. And you have every right."

If he had ever felt more like scum in his life, he couldn't remember it. Shame made him drop his head, his forehead resting on her arm. She was so brave and so strong, and he had hurt her by not reassuring her from the outset that he didn't hold her responsible.

"Oh, Bailey. I don't deserve you. What a jackass I am, my love. I've been angry at the world and scared out of my mind and weaving on my feet with fatigue. But I should have realized you would feel this way. You're so very conscientious. I don't blame you. I would *never* blame you. I know you would protect Cade with your life."

She stroked his hair, a tentative, tender caress that was evidence of her generous spirit. "You're not just saying that to make me feel better?"

He sat up and stared at her sternly. "The kidnapping could have happened if he had been with me. Now stop worrying."

"I won't stop worrying until we have some good news."

"Is it good news to hear that I love you?"

She paled. "You're delirious."

"Not in the slightest. Tired, yes. And frightened for you and my son, yes. But completely in my right mind. I was all set to propose when things went south."

She stared at him, mute.

"I didn't think it would be such a shock," he said. "Surely you knew we were headed in this direction."

She shook her head. "No. I thought we were breaking up."

He grinned despite his exhaustion. "Well, think again. I want you in my life. I need you and Cade needs you."

"I don't think I can talk about this yet. It feels wrong."

He sobered. "I understand. But don't make me stay away from you. I can't bear that on top of everything else."

Her bottom lip quivered as she reached out to grip his hand with hers. "He's coming back to us. We have to believe that."

Gil's cell phone vibrated in his pocket, startling him. He answered it, his heart in his throat. Two minutes later, he hung up, his eyes damp. Inhaling a harsh breath, he leaned over and kissed Bailey…hard. "Nate's team has found Cade," he said, his voice gruff.

Her lips opened and closed. Tears trickled from her beautiful eyes. "He's okay?"

"Completely." He shuddered, swamped by a wave of relief so strong it made him dizzy. "My in-laws were hiding out with him in Del Rio, hoping to slip across the border into Mexico when the furor died down."

"Poor little man. He must be so confused."

"We'll make sure he sees a counselor. And we'll smother him with love." He nudged her hip. "Move over, gorgeous." He raised the head of the bed and leaned back against the pillows, gathering her in his right arm, tucking her against his chest. "Nate is driving him back to Royal early in the morning. I want you to be there with me at the Straight Arrow, Bailey, to welcome him home. If the doctor thinks you're well enough to be released."

She nestled into his embrace. "Oh, yes," she said. "I wouldn't miss it for the world."

Eight hours later, Bailey sat on Gil's front porch wrapped in a quilt, waiting for Nate's squad car to come into sight. When it did, she stood up, the tears flowing again. She hated feeling so weak and emotional, but her relief and joy were profound.

Gil put a hand on her shoulder. "Save your strength, honey. I'll bring him to you."

The car pulled to a stop at the foot of the steps, and a door flew open. "Daddy!" Cade ran toward his father, the two males meeting halfway in a boisterous hug that was beautiful to watch. Seeing Gil reunited with his son healed a deep crack in Bailey's heart. She may not have solved the case of Alex's kidnapping, but that failure paled in comparison to this victory.

Moments later she saw Gil whisper something in Cade's ear. The child looked up and saw Bailey. His mouth rounded in an *O* of surprise and his little face crumpled. "Miss Bailey," he wailed, running up the remainder of the steps. "You're okay." He threw himself at her, and Bailey winced as she tried to catch him without jarring her injury.

Hugging Cade tightly, she rested her cheek against his dark hair. "I'm pretty tough," she said. "And you were awfully brave."

Gil eased his son away. "We have to be careful with Miss Bailey, Cade. Her head is still getting well."

After that, Cade insisted on seeing her bandages, and of course, they all had to thank Nate profusely. It was almost an hour later before she was finally alone with Gil. Cade had run to his room to play with his toys. His father scooped Bailey into his arms and carried her up the stairs to his bedroom. She could hear the steady beat of his heart beneath her cheek.

"You smell good," she said, burrowing her nose in the crisply starched fabric of his white cotton shirt. In honor of Cade's homecoming, he had worn his best Stetson and his fanciest pair of cowboy boots.

Gil flipped back the quilt and the top sheet and laid her gently on the soft mattress. "Don't flirt with me," he begged. "I'm trying to remind myself that your recovery has a long way to go."

"I want to sleep with you tonight," she whispered.

A dark flush tinged his cheekbones. "Sleep only. I won't be responsible for putting you back in the hospital."

She tugged his hand. "Lie down beside me."

He kicked off his boots, removed his belt, and stretched out on his back, careful not to jostle her head. He closed his eyes and breathed deeply. "I feel so damn good, I may just float up to the ceiling."

Linking her fingers with his, she smiled up at the surface in question. "I'd miss you," she said.

After a long silence, he spoke again, this time with no humor at all in his voice. "I've been waiting to hear you say something very important, Bailey."

She froze, the words stuck in her throat. It was a huge commitment. Turning her life upside down.

Giving up everything she knew. "You're asking if I love you?"

"Yes."

Why was it that she could face down an armed assailant without flinching, but taking this leap petrified her? She'd been on her own for a long time. Self-reliant. Depending on no one. Her emotionally unavailable father had taught her that.

But Gil Addison was an entirely different kind of parent. And an entirely different kind of man. He cared. And he wasn't afraid to show it.

The question was, could she be as brave? She turned on her side and put a hand on his chest, covering his heart. "I do care about you, Gil. How could I not?"

Her wording was not lost on him, because he grimaced. "Thank God. For a while there, I thought you only wanted me for sex."

She laughed softly. "Well, that *is* a definite plus."

He lifted up on his elbow, head propped on his hand. His crooked smile was the kind of thing that made good girls get in trouble. "As flattering as that is to hear, I want more than your luscious body. I know we have problems to sort out, but we'll manage it. I love you, sweetheart, heart and soul and everything in between. I want to make a family with you and Cade. I realize you probably didn't bargain for getting hitched to a guy with a kid. But he's a pretty great kid, and he adores you."

"I adore *him,* but are you absolutely sure about this marriage idea?"

"One hundred percent. I know you're very good at your job, but maybe Nate could use you here in Royal. Alex still doesn't remember anything, and del Toro is throwing his weight around with no real success. Even in an unofficial capacity, your skills would be important. You'd be the one doing the sacrificing. I get that. And I know it's not fair. But the Straight Arrow is Cade's birth-right."

Even though her head throbbed and she felt weak, her heart soared. "I wouldn't mind learning how to be Cade's mom. That would keep me plenty busy for a while."

"Is that a yes?" His hand toyed with the buttons on her blouse, his thumb brushing her nipple through the fabric.

A sweet trickle of arousal swam in her veins, making her light-headed and giddy. "All the single women in town will be gunning for me if I lasso Royal's most eligible bachelor," she teased.

"You can take them," he said. "I have faith in you."

She searched his face, wanting desperately to believe she had found her happy ending. "You won't change your mind? It might be the endorphins talking."

He nudged her to her back again and laid his head on her flat belly, his fingers stroking the center seam of her soft khaki pants. "I've never been more sure of anything in my life. Would you mind terribly if we made a few babies together?"

She smiled, though he couldn't see. "It might take a lot of effort on your part." His intimate touch made her shiver.

"I think I can handle it. But we have one more hurdle, Bailey. One glaring omission. When a man lays his heart on the line, it seems like he's entitled to a little sweet talk in return."

"I see."

"But only if you mean it." He sat up, one knee raised, and stared at her with some anxiety. "I know I'm pushing you…taking advantage of you in a vulnerable condition. But I…"

She put a hand over his mouth, her gaze intent. "I do love you, Gil Addison. For now and forever. Come here and kiss me."

As kisses went, it was a doozy. Deep and wet and hungry. They were both breathless when it ended, and a certain part of Gil's anatomy was hard as stone.

He stared down at her, dark eyes flashing. "How long until those stitches come out?"

"Seven more days, give or take."

"Can you plan a wedding in seven days?"

"People will think we *have* to get married," she said, daring to tease him when he was primed for action.

He lifted her hand to his lips, his handsome face solemn. "We *do* have to get married," he said softly. "Because I'm not willing to live another minute without you in my life and in my bed."

Bailey blinked, totally undone by the sight of this rough and tough cowboy baring his soul to her. "Then I believe my answer is yes, dear Gil. Because I feel the same way. There's just one more thing…"

One wicked eyebrow lifted. "Yes, my love?"
"On our wedding night, I want you to wear the Stetson to bed…"

And as it happens…he did.

* * * * *

Discover more romance at

www.millsandboon.co.uk

- ❤ WIN great prizes in our exclusive competitions

- ❤ BUY new titles before they hit the shops

- ❤ BROWSE new books and REVIEW your favourites

- ❤ SAVE on new books with the Mills & Boon® Bookclub™

- ❤ DISCOVER new authors

PLUS, to chat about your favourite reads, get the latest news and find special offers:

- Find us on facebook.com/millsandboon
- Follow us on twitter.com/millsandboonuk
- ❤ Sign up to our newsletter at millsandboon.co.uk